◄JOYCE WOLF, ►1949 –

Between the Cracks

Dial Books for Young Readers
New York

Published by Dial Books for Young Readers
A Division of Penguin Books USA Inc.
375 Hudson Street
New York, New York 10014

Library of Congress Cataloging in Publication Data
Wolf, Joyce, 1949–
Between the cracks / by Joyce Wolf.
p. cm.
Summary: When Bentley's friend Cal falls under the spell of
an evil wizard, she risks her life to help him.
ISBN 0-8037-1270-7 (tr).
[1. Wizards—Fiction. 2. Friendship—Fiction.] I. Title.
PZ7.W81916Be 1992 [Fic]—dc20 92-2661 CIP AC

To Bonnie, Vanessa, Zak,
Ann, and most of all,
to Tim

1

It was the first really hot day of summer. Bentley was sitting on a swing in Laurel Park, evaluating the tan on her thin brown legs, kicking up dust and waiting for Charles and Cal, when she heard the little kid scream. The scream sounded more angry than anything else, but it made her look around for the source of the noise.

The first thing she saw was Todd Lunden and that was enough to explain it.

Todd was just starting eighth grade in the fall, even though he was almost fifteen. He was taller, bigger, and meaner than anybody else in Lincoln Junior High. Bentley had gone through seventh grade with him last year and she knew all about him, but so far she'd gotten through life without ever having to come face-to-face with him. Now Todd was hanging off the top of the monkey bars acting like King Kong and tormenting some little kid. He was dangling the kid's fire engine out of reach and making ape noises while the little kid screamed and jumped for it.

Bentley looked around to see if the little boy had a brother or a parent or somebody to take care of him. But there was nobody.

"Nuts." Bentley was the only responsible person around. She twirled a strand of her shoulder-length brown hair in her fingers, then started to chew the end of it.

The kid's screams changed from anger to misery.

"Nuts," Bentley said again as she slipped off the swing and began to move slowly toward the monkey bars. It wasn't any of her business. The kid wasn't actually getting hurt, and Todd was bound to get tired of the whole thing soon. But she couldn't just sit there and listen to the kid scream. That would be dishonorable. Ignoble, Bentley thought. Good word.

Bentley got to the edge of the circle of packed dirt that surrounded the monkey bars and scowled at the little kid. His cheeks were wet with tears and his nose was running. His eyes were screwed tightly shut.

She looked up at Todd leering and making faces from the top of the monkey bars. He looked huge.

"Why don't you just give him back his stupid fire engine?" Bentley said.

"Nyye-e-e-a-a-h-h-h!" Todd bobbed up and down on the iron bars. "Try and make me! I'll give you a black eye just like Julie Bell!"

Julie Bell was thirteen and a half, a year older than Bentley. Todd had punched her in the face last May, and Julie's right eye had been black, green, and purple for two weeks.

Bentley meant to say something brave and defiant to Todd, but instead she found herself taking a step backward.

Then a voice spoke suddenly beside her, making Bentley jump.

"What's going on?" It was Cal, quiet as a sliver of moonlight.

"Nothing!" Bentley said quickly. Cal was bound to want to rescue the kid, and that would only mean worse trouble.

Todd laughed and shook the truck. The little kid howled and cried harder.

"Give him back his truck," Cal said softly.

Todd sneered down at them. "Who's gonna make me? *You?* I could turn *you* into dog food!"

Cal was lean, wiry, and tall for almost thirteen, but he was much smaller than Todd. With his gray-green eyes, and white-blond hair, Cal always reminded Bentley of a tiger. He had a tiger's kind of fierceness too, Bentley thought. The problem was that ever since last year, Cal refused to fight.

Cal moved onto the hard-packed dirt. "Give him the truck."

"He probably weighs fifty pounds more than you!" Bentley said.

"I know."

Bentley groaned. Cal hadn't hit anyone since he'd broken Stuart Engelman's nose last year in a fight that Stuart, who was bigger and older, had started. Cal said he didn't want to hurt anyone ever again.

"This is stupid!" Bentley said as Cal walked toward Todd. "It's *futile!*" Good word.

But Cal moved the little kid aside and stood in front of Todd with one hand held out for the toy. Without any warning, Todd swung down and used the heavy, wooden fire truck to punch Cal hard in the stomach. Cal fell into the dust with a noise like *oof.*

Bentley flinched and bit her bottom lip. Do something! she scolded herself. But she kept seeing Julie Bell's black eye, and she couldn't move.

Todd kept punching and kicking him, but Cal refused to hit back. He blocked most of the blows, but still he got knocked down two more times. Every time he fell, Cal got back up and held out his hand for the truck.

Cal was getting up for the third time when Bentley noticed the bearded man in black standing in the shadow of the trees, watching them. Why didn't he do something to stop it? But it seemed to her the dark man was smiling as he watched.

Finally Todd stopped. "You're weird," he said to Cal. "Just too weird." Todd let the truck drop into the dust at Cal's feet. "See ya later, bozo!" He loped away across the deserted baseball diamond and out of the park.

The little kid ran up, snatched his fire truck, and took off at a dead run. Bentley watched the kid go, ashamed to look at Cal. She had let him down. She hadn't even tried to help.

"Hey!" It was Charles yelling cheerfully at them

from across the park. A moment later he came riding up on his old clunker bike with ribbons and decorations flying.

He braked to a stop at the monkey bars in a cloud of dust. "What's up?" Charles turned his grin from Bentley to Cal and back again.

"Not much," Cal said.

"Cal just helped some little kid and got beaten up by Todd Lunden," Bentley announced. "And it was all my fault. I got him into it and then I didn't help."

"I didn't need help," Cal said. "And you didn't get me into it." He brushed dirt off the seat of his shorts. "And I didn't get beaten up."

Charles's eyebrows rose and disappeared beneath the thick, straight honey-colored hair that hung over his forehead. "Yes, yes!" he said. "Swami Charles sees all. The honorable Cal the Defender will always fight for truth and justice! He makes his stand for the innocent and the underdog!"

"He kept getting knocked down!"

Charles nodded. "Face it, Bentley. Cal Nicholas is a born good guy, and getting knocked down is just part of the job."

"It's not like that! I'm not a good guy at all!" Cal jammed his fists into the pockets of his shorts. "That's why I wouldn't hit Todd Lunden back. I couldn't do it because what I really wanted to do was smash his dumb face. If I let myself hit him, I don't know what I'd do to him. Look, I never told you this, but I felt great when I broke Stuart Engelman's nose! And that was *awful*."

Charles shrugged. "That proves it. You don't even want to hurt a doughnuthead like Todd Lunden. See? You are a good guy. Don't worry so much. Why don't we just go to my house and play Mille Bornes?"

The card game was a corny old Donovan family tradition they all complained about and played anyway. Bentley and Cal were partners against Charles and his older brother Arthur. But the afternoon was hot and lazy and no one was really concentrating on the game as they sprawled on the grass in the Donovans' backyard. It was Bentley's turn, and she laid a hazard card on top of the Donovans' pile.

"A challenge!" Charles declared, rubbing his hands together. But just then his mom called a five-minute warning for the boys. In five minutes, Arthur would be responsible for getting two-year-old James Francis Donovan to lie down and take a nap. That was practically a superhuman feat.

"What do you think?" Charles asked Arthur. "Should we use your five minutes to blitz these two?"

Arthur considered the question, then shook his head and tossed in his cards. "I think I'll do some wind sprints." He sprang to his feet and trotted off.

"I thought Arthur was more the intellectual type." Cal was watching tall, skinny Arthur take a runner's crouch in the front yard to dash down Colter Street.

"He's expanding his horizons." Charles gathered up all their cards to deal a new game for the three of them. "Let's put some life into it, people!"

But this game went even more slowly than the last,

and no one was concentrating. Bentley was lying on her stomach in the grass, brooding about Cal and Todd Lunden and what a coward she had been. Faint-hearted. Lily-livered. A milksop. Such good words and such a rotten feeling. She pressed her nose into her forearm and inhaled the warm, sun-baked smell while her hair made a tent around her face. Next time, she vowed to herself. Next time I get the chance I'm going to be brave and true.

She glanced at Charles. He was crouched over something in the grass, watching intently. Bentley sat up and moved closer, curious about what he had found. Charles was always finding something that he thought was fascinating. It was probably a bug. Charles liked bugs.

"Whose turn is it?" Bentley asked, although she didn't actually care.

"Cal's." Charles looked over at him, then made a face. "Geez. He's doing it again."

Bentley sat up. Nuts. It gave her a creepy feeling to see Cal like that.

"Hey, Cal!" Charles said. "Wake up!"

Cal didn't answer. He was sitting cross-legged in the grass with his cards lying loose in his lap and a blank, dreamy look on his face.

"Cal?" She raised her voice and made it sharp. "Are you sick or something?"

Cal blinked, shook himself, and brushed at his face as if he'd just walked through a spider's web. "What? Were you talking to me?"

Charles considered him curiously. "You looked

like you were taking a nap with your eyes open. *Again.*"

Bentley was chewing her thumbnail. "More like a zombie. Why do you keep doing that?"

Cal scowled at her. "Can we just skip it?"

Bentley couldn't remember exactly when Cal had started having these odd trances, but they were definitely getting worse. He was having more and more of them. And he was doing other weird things. Sometimes he'd jump and look over his shoulder as if somebody was talking to him when there was nobody there. Or he'd be holding a book or a ball or a sandwich and suddenly drop it as if it had tried to bite him. But he wouldn't talk about any of it.

"I've gotta go," Cal announced. He tossed his cards down and stood up.

"Me too!" Bentley decided to go with him. Maybe if they were alone she could get him to tell her what was going on. At least she could try.

She was wondering what she could say to Cal to persuade him to talk when Cal solved the problem himself.

"Do you believe in ghosts?" he asked in a rush as they walked down the Donovans' driveway. "Because, the thing is, I think I'm being haunted."

"Haunted?" Bentley stopped walking and stared at him.

Cal looked embarrassed. "I see this face. It's a man that I see *everywhere*. Even in impossible places. He's there and then he's gone! I dream about him too. All the time! I don't know who he is. I just call him The Dark Man."

"Does he have a beard?" Bentley thought of the man under the trees, watching Cal and smiling.

"Yes!" Cal's eyes lit up. "How did you know?"

"He was in the park. This morning."

"You *saw* him?"

Bentley nodded. It was strange, she thought now, how The Dark Man had suddenly been there. She hadn't seen him coming, and she hadn't seen him leave. But he was gone when Charles arrived. "He was smiling," Bentley said. "Not a very nice smile."

"That's him!" Cal said. "That's my ghost!"

2

"A *ghost*! You're not really serious, are you?"

"I knew it would sound crazy." Cal turned away. "Never mind, okay? Just forget I said anything."

"But The Dark Man can't be a ghost if I saw him too. Can he?"

"Then it's probably a different guy. Anyway, it's my problem." Cal shifted restlessly from foot to foot. "I'm gonna run home. See you later." He took off like a racehorse when the starting gate opens, streaking down Colter Street and out of sight.

Rats! Bentley watched him in dismay. Why didn't I just listen and keep my mouth shut!

But *ghosts*! Bentley started the walk home slowly. Ghosts. Did she believe in them? Could Cal really be haunted? She turned the idea over all the way home without finding an answer.

Bentley let herself into her house with a key she and

her mom kept hidden in a fake rock by the door. She didn't expect her mom to be home. So the weird noises that came drifting downstairs were a shock.

Bwong-bwong-bwong. Bwong-bwong-bwong. And underneath that sound was a low humming that seemed to vibrate deep in the marrow of her bones.

What if there *were* ghosts? And what if now *she* was being haunted? Bentley stood frozen in the front hall, listening.

She heard a hollow *click-click-click* like the rhythm sticks kids played in kindergarten. And somebody began to sing. Or that's what Bentley figured the noise must be. What it really sounded like, Bentley thought, was a bunch of Munchkins. And the Munchkins were all chanting *yam-yam-yam*.

But there was something familiar about the strange singing and rhythmic sounds. They made her think of lost tribes in some adventure movie or in *National Geographic* specials.

"Uncle Rudy!" Bentley suddenly yelled and launched herself at full gallop up the stairs. "Hey!"

She crashed into him when he emerged from the extra bedroom, and they ended up tangled together, hugging and thumping each other and grinning a lot. Like a couple of dancing bears, Bentley thought with her cheeks tight and round from smiling so hard, except that I only come up to his chest and Uncle Rudy is red-haired and skinny as a stick.

"A beard!" she shrieked. "You grew a beard!"

"And you've grown at least two inches since the last time I saw you!" Uncle Rudy said.

They stepped back to look each other over, and Bentley wondered if her grin looked as goofy as his did. He looked even more rumpled than usual, she decided. He was wearing wrinkled khaki shorts and a wrinkled shirt and his red hair was standing on end.

"Does Mom know you're here?" Bentley asked.

"Nope. I only recently decided to descend on you. I let myself in with my permanent-guest key." Uncle Rudy absentmindedly stirred his hair up some more. "I came straight from the outback. Twenty-two hours on assorted airplanes, limos, buses, and taxis, and here I am."

"But we didn't know you were coming!" Whenever he visited before, Uncle Rudy always wrote weeks ahead to tell them exactly when he'd be in town. Fair warning, he always said.

"I guess you'd call it a spur-of-the-moment detour on an unscheduled trip," he told her. "There I was, happy as a hedgehog in Borroloola when suddenly it seemed like a good idea to take a leave from the field and check in at the department. And since the university is so near, I thought I'd take the opportunity to pay a visit to my favorite sister and favorite niece."

Bentley's mom was Uncle Rudy's only sister and she was his only niece. It was an old joke, but Bentley still liked it. Probably because she liked Uncle Rudy so much, almost any dumb joke was funny.

"Then is your project done?" Bentley asked. Those weird noises coming from the bedroom must be Uncle Rudy's field tapes. They weren't Munchkins, they were Australian aboriginals chanting.

"Not if I can help it." Uncle Rudy said it in a tight-lipped way that didn't sound like him at all.

"Doesn't Dr. Gardner want you to finish it?" Bentley knew Dr. Gardner was her uncle's boss and friend and head of the anthropology department at the university where Uncle Rudy taught.

"Ah-h-h-h," Uncle Rudy sighed. "Gardner."

Now *that* sounded significant, Bentley thought, appraising his face.

There were wrinkled pouches under Uncle Rudy's red-rimmed eyes, and his eyelids were puffy and droopy. He's really tired, Bentley decided, but that's not all. There's something wrong, something that's making him sad.

It was all mysterious and unsettling. Uncle Rudy was never sad, and he never made surprise visits from someplace as far away as Australia.

"What about Dr. Gardner?" Bentley asked.

Usually Uncle Rudy's whole face lit up when he talked about Dr. Gardner. But not now. Now he just frowned.

"Is something wrong? I thought you liked him a lot."

"Yes," Uncle Rudy said. "I do." Then he yawned an enormous yawn that seemed to take him by surprise. He blinked at Bentley like a sleepy owl.

"Why don't you take a nap?" Bentley said. It seemed like a sensible thing for him to do. "I'll tell Mom you're here when she gets home, and you can talk to her later."

"Good idea. I think the jet lag just caught up with

me." He yawned again and gave Bentley another hug. "See you later, kiddo." Uncle Rudy ducked back into the guest bedroom, closing the door behind him.

"Pleasant dreams," Bentley said.

The door swung open again. "Look on the hall table," Uncle Rudy said and winked before he disappeared again.

Bentley ran down the stairs to the front hall. There on the table, next to the phone, was a package the size of a shoe box wrapped in brown paper. *Miss Phillipa Bentley* was written on it in black Magic Marker. Her name didn't seem quite as awful when it was written out, Bentley thought. Of course, almost no one actually called her Phillipa.

She picked up the shoe box and shook it gently. Something large, soft, and heavy shifted inside it.

Bentley had just begun carefully unwrapping the package when the front door burst open.

"Good! You're here! Take the milk, will you, please?" Bentley's mom stood in the doorway with her arms wrapped around two bulging grocery bags. She had a plastic jug of milk hanging from one finger.

Bentley hurried to grab the milk and trotted beside her mom as they rushed to the kitchen.

"There's more in the car," her mom said, thumping the bags down on the kitchen table.

"Uncle Rudy's here!" Bentley announced.

"Rudy? He's here now?"

"He's in the purple bedroom, asleep." It was lavender, but Bentley liked the word purple better.

"Is he all right?"

"I guess so."

"Did he say why he's here?"

"Just visiting on his way to the university."

"Did he finish his research? Why didn't he let us know he was coming?" Her mom seemed just as puzzled by Uncle Rudy's mysterious appearance as Bentley was.

"I don't know," Bentley said. She remembered the complicated way he had said Dr. Gardner's name. "I think it might have something to do with Dr. Gardner."

"Hmm." Her mom thought about it. "Dr. Gardner is quite old. In his late seventies or eighties, I think."

"Uncle Rudy always says he's a foxy old coot," Bentley said. "Sapient." Full of wisdom. Good word.

"I hope he's not ill," Bentley's mom said. Then her face brightened. "But . . . an egg is not a chicken. Right?"

Sometimes her mom's sayings took some puzzling over, and Bentley worked on that one as she followed her mom to the car. It must have something to do with not counting your chickens before they were hatched, she decided.

Together Bentley and her mom brought in the last of the bags and began distributing cans, boxes, frozen food, deli and take-out containers to the fridge, freezer, and cabinets.

"Chinese tonight from Wonton Charlie's!" Bentley's mom announced. "Moo Goo Gai Pan! Three

Delicacies Delight, Sub Gum Chop Suey, and egg rolls!''

Bentley sighed. They never ate normal food like other people. At Charles's house they ate things like pork chops and mashed potatoes and green beans. Or meat loaf. Or macaroni and cheese. Food you could recognize.

"What's the Moo Goo stuff?" Bentley cautiously sniffed one of the white cartons. The smell was warm and mysterious. Well, Bentley thought, maybe I could eat a little of it.

"Chicken. You had it before and you like it." Her mom began emptying the cartons into serving bowls. "I've got to eat and run. Did you remember that this is one of my Belle nights?"

"Oh." Bentley had forgotten her mom would be out for the evening. "Belle" was short for *Automo-Belle*. It was a costume her mom had made, a dress with a kind of giant hoopskirt. Except that the skirt was shaped and decorated to look like an old-fashioned red touring car. And her mom stuck out of the top of the Belle wearing a duster coat, hat, and goggles, as if she were the driver.

Creative Costumes, Inc., was one of her mom's best businesses. People would hire her to walk around in the Belle at events, and sometimes she'd talk about automobile history. She went to conventions for car dealers and car insurance salespeople, and to parties raising money for charity. She had other costumes too. When she was little, Bentley's favorite was Big

Mo, the giant hot dog. Then there was Albert, the talking Christmas tree.

"Set the table and come back in ten minutes. Okay?" Bentley's mom opened a cabinet and began clanking through their pots and pans, looking faintly puzzled, as if she'd never seen them before.

"Paper or foam?"

"Soggy stuff. Go for foam," Bentley's mom directed. It was only on rare occasions when they ate off real plates. Setting the dining room table only took a minute. That left Bentley nine more minutes to open Uncle Rudy's package.

She took the package carefully, and with a feeling of ceremony, from the hall table. She carried the brown paper package into the living room and sat on the floor to unwrap it.

There was a layer of newspaper under the brown wrapping. It was the front page of a paper from a town called Alice Springs, and Bentley laid the newspaper aside to read later. Under all the wrappings was a shoe box.

Bentley eased the lid off, cautious about what might happen next. With a package from Uncle Rudy, you never knew what might come flying out.

Inside the box, the first thing Bentley saw was a piece of brightly colored fabric. It folded around and cushioned something heavy and big as a grapefruit, wrapped in more newspaper. And there was something smaller, wrapped in newspaper and tucked into a corner of the box.

She unfolded the bright cloth. It was a large square of thin, soft cotton batik patterned in bold earth colors. Rich red clay. Berry purple. Golden yellows and dusty wildflower blues. There were little figures of people and animals and a graceful pattern of lines and dots.

The small packet in the corner of the box held a seashell strung on a blue silk cord. The shell was long, flat, and about the size of her palm. One side was rough and gray, but the inside of the shell was iridescent as a pearl and had a carving on it. It was a maze, Bentley realized. And inside the maze was a trail of tiny bare footprints leading to the puzzle center. Bentley traced the footprints with one finger, smiling at the way the feet seemed to be hurrying along.

She saved the round, heavy thing until last, unwrapping it slowly. It was a rough, red clay pot sealed with cloudy gray wax, and there was a note attached.

> *Wait for me!*
> *Love,*
> *Uncle Rudy*

It must be something special, Bentley decided. Something Uncle Rudy would want to watch her open and tell her some story about. Uncle Rudy was like that.

She couldn't wait for him to wake up.

3

The Moo Goo stuff wasn't bad, Bentley decided as she and her mom finished dinner in the dining room. Bentley planned to add it to her list of "acceptable foods." The list was Cal's idea. Bentley would present it to her mom as a kind of security measure so, hopefully, she wouldn't get stuck eating raw fish or something else disgusting her mom might bring home. A person needed security about basic things like food.

"What did you do today?" Bentley's mom asked as she bent over her plate. She began using her chopsticks to scoop up mouthfuls of chop suey and rice, and paused to smile encouragingly. Mrs. Bentley was in a hurry to get to her Belle night at the Elks Club, but she was always a good listener.

With a pang, Bentley remembered her cowardice in standing by and watching Todd Lunden knock Cal down again and again. And she thought of how she answered Cal's weird question about ghosts. She had let Cal down again, Bentley thought, by not listening when he tried to talk to her. Suddenly she wasn't hungry anymore.

"Not much." Bentley began pushing all the ingredients in her Three Delicacies Delight into separate piles with her fork. She could feel her mom watching her. The chopsticks weren't moving anymore.

"Bad day at Black Rock?"

Bentley shrugged. She was ashamed to tell her mom what a wimp she had been. Her mom would have *done* something. She always said, "A woman alone has to stand on her own two feet and fight her own battles." But so far, Bentley had never really managed to stand up for herself. Cal kept saying Bentley had courage and all sorts of qualities she didn't even know about yet. But she figured he was just being nice to her. Defending the underdog. That's how they got to be friends a year and a half ago when Cal transferred into Bentley's class.

Mrs. Stone had called on her to read a poem out loud. Bentley loved words and poems and the rhythms of language and really liked to read out loud. But Joanne Glass and Tracey Walters, who thought they were totally superior and always had to pick on somebody, started groaning and snickering and making rude noises. "Let her read," Cal had said. "She's got a flair for it." Cal was new, but he was good-looking, smart, and athletic. Joanne and Tracey had shut up. And Bentley and Cal had been friends ever since.

Cal always stood up for her. And now Bentley had let him down twice in one day.

"Want to talk about it?" her mom asked.

Bentley shook her head.

"Anything you can do to change it?"

Bentley started to shake her head again, then stopped. She *could* tell Cal she was sorry and try to get him talking again. And this time she would promise to really listen. "Maybe."

Bentley's mom jumped up and began gathering dishes and silverware. "I've got to go—but remember this: Failure only defeats the traveler who cannot see another path!"

"Sure, Mom." That was one of her mom's favorite sayings. Bentley liked sayings that were easier to understand, like "Tomorrow is another day." That's what Scarlett O'Hara said in *Gone with the Wind*. Tomorrow, first thing in the morning, Bentley decided, she was going to call Cal and find out all about his ghost. The Dark Man.

Bentley went to bed early and didn't see her mom or Uncle Rudy again until the next morning. They were already at the kitchen table, talking and drinking coffee, when Bentley came downstairs. But they stopped talking as soon as they saw her standing in the doorway, and there was an uncomfortable moment of silence. Uncle Rudy looked less rumpled and tired, Bentley thought, but his hair was still standing on end. And her mom was absentmindedly patting him on the arm.

There really *was* something wrong, Bentley decided. "Hi," she said, feeling awkward.

Then Uncle Rudy grinned at her, and Bentley felt a rush of gladness just to see him there, even if there were problems.

"Hi, yourself!" he said.

"Well!" Bentley's mom stood up. She put her hand on Uncle Rudy's shoulder and squeezed it. "It's a Bentley Realty day, and I've actually got three new prospects! Someone to look at my poor old houses."

"Treasures," Bentley corrected her.

"You're right." Her mom brushed crumbs off the soft sea-green jacket that she wore for "important meetings." "The home buyer with imagination sees beyond the sometimes neglected exterior of a Bentley home. They see the potential for greatness in a house just waiting for the right owner! And with Bentley Realty, the buyer who has a deeper, clearer vision may find a hidden treasure!"

"Bravo!" Uncle Rudy cried. He and Bentley both applauded loudly.

"And now I'm late! Good-bye!" Bentley's mom kissed Uncle Rudy and then Bentley. "Sweetheart," she said to Bentley, "make sure you eat some breakfast and take a vitamin."

"Mm-hm." Her mom thought any nutritional requirements that Chinese food, squid, carrot sticks, Some Guys Pizza, and Delano's Deli didn't cover could be taken care of by vitamins. Mrs. Riggs, the home ec teacher at Lincoln, would probably be quite dismayed. Good word.

"See you, Kate," Uncle Rudy said as Bentley's mom waved at them both from the doorway.

You didn't have to look too closely to tell they were brother and sister, Bentley decided, studying her red-headed uncle. He was lightly tanned with a sprinkle of freckles across the bridge of his nose, and his eyes were a warm hazel. Bentley's mom was much smaller and more compact. Kate Bentley called her hair auburn even though it wasn't much redder than Bentley's brown hair. Auburn sounded dramatic. And her mom was pretty, Bentley knew. Animated. Good word. And the sparkle that was so lively in her mom's face showed up as a deep glow and a twinkle in Uncle Rudy's eyes.

"I hope you're not going to tell me I have food stuck in my beard," Uncle Rudy said after Bentley had been studying his face for some time.

"Yuck!"

"You had that kind of look on your face." Uncle Rudy brushed at his beard and grinned at her.

"Have you eaten yet?" Bentley asked. "I could cook breakfast." She opened a kitchen cabinet to look for something nutritionally sound and well-balanced. "Pancakes?"

"My stomach is still in a different time zone. I had breakfast at four this morning, and now I'm just stalling, waiting for an early lunch."

"Maybe tomorrow," Bentley said.

"Maybe," Uncle Rudy said. "Or the day after. I may be around for a while."

Well, that was a clue, Bentley thought. And good news. She loved having Uncle Rudy around. But why was he here? She wanted to ask, but hesitated.

The unmilked cow, her mom always said, is happier to see the farmer. Maybe if she waited, Uncle Rudy would tell her about it on his own. Bentley helped herself to some fortified health food cereal and joined her uncle at the table. At least she could ask him about his project.

Uncle Rudy had written to them regularly about his project and about the people he worked with and knew. Now she could ask him to fill her in on the news since his last letter.

So Uncle Rudy talked about Maggie Winmati and her new baby, about old Toby Matinga and how he finally let a dentist pull his bad tooth, and how Toby's son Harry had finally come back after six months in Humpty Doo.

Bentley always loved Uncle Rudy's stories. She could feel the world grow bigger just listening to the names of the places he'd seen. There was Nourlangie Rock near Jabiru in the northern part of the territory. There were towns called Katherine and Utopia and Bradshaw's Run and places called Borroloola, Larrimah, and Yuendumu. When Uncle Rudy said the words, Bentley silently shaped the sounds with him, loving the way they felt on her lips and tongue.

"And how's The Rock?" Bentley asked.

"Mysterious as always." Ayers Rock was where Uncle Rudy had his project. Throughout the area for hundreds of miles, the aboriginal tribes just called it The Rock. As if it were the only rock there was. Uluru. It had been a sacred place for thousands of years.

"Hey!" Uncle Rudy said. "What about my package?"

"It was wonderful! Very *illuminating*." Good word. To Bentley the shell necklace, with its maze and tiny footprints, and the batik scarf had seemed like gentle clues to another kind of life. "And nothing exploded! But what about the clay pot? Can we open it now?"

"I thought you'd never ask!"

Bentley ran up to her room to get the little pot. Uncle Rudy was right behind her, his long legs taking the stairs three at a time. He was looking for a cassette tape, he told Bentley, for "mood music." They would rendezvous at the dining room table.

When Bentley came downstairs, Uncle Rudy was spreading newspaper on the table to protect its polished surface. He put his tape on the stereo, and Bentley heard again the strange sounds and voices that had announced Uncle Rudy yesterday.

"What did you think of the music?" he asked.

Bentley had the perfect description. "I was transfixed."

The clicking and roaring, chanting and droning voices came from speakers all around them. It filled the room with strange, chattering people and a sense of wild power. Uncle Rudy took the round clay pot and seated himself at the head of the table while Bentley took a chair at his right.

As Bentley watched, Uncle Rudy chose a short, broad blade from his Swiss Army knife to slip between the cloudy wax seal and the earthen jar. He began to pry gently around the rim of the jar, breaking the seal. And as he worked, Uncle Rudy told her about the Dreamtime.

Spirits walked the earth in those days, he said. They were the Ancestors who rose from the ground. And as they walked, they dreamed, creating the mountains, lakes, land, animals, and people.

Uncle Rudy told Bentley about the Dreaming Trails and the spirits of the Eagle Hawk, the Moon, the Spirit Snake, and others. He told her how, at the end of the Dreamtime, the spirits returned to the earth, becoming one with it.

The knife's broad blade had made the full circle around the mouth of the pot. Now Uncle Rudy used the blade to ease the wax seal free.

Bentley held her breath and leaned to look closer.

"The earth," Uncle Rudy said as he shook some of the treasure from inside the pot into the palm of his hand. He was shaking out a handful of dust. The dust in the pot was a deep rust red, as old as time, baked dry in a desert at the heart of the world. Like blood, Bentley thought. Earth blood. She felt as if Uncle Rudy were giving her the essence of that mystical place on the other side of the world.

"The dust is called red ocher," Uncle Rudy said.

"The aboriginals believe it holds and symbolizes the power of the land and the spirits."

Bentley stroked the silky softness of the dust. It was a wonderful present.

"The dust can be a way to touch the spirits, a way to summon magical protection. Earth magic."

As Uncle Rudy gazed at the red dust in his hand, it seemed as if he were traveling back to the desert, back to the mystery of Uluru, The Rock. Then he cleared his throat. "The dust is actually a red ocher pigment used for painting almost anything. Pictures on cloth or bark or stone. Or even on yourself."

Bentley stared at the small mound of deep red pigment in his palm. Earth magic. It was going to be important, she thought with a shiver. "Red ocher," she said softly. "Magic."

"It seemed right for you," Uncle Rudy said.

The sound of the telephone made them both jump. Bentley hurried to answer it.

"Bentley?" It was Cal. His voice was humming with excitement. "I think I just saw The Dark Man go into a store on Locust Street. Can you meet me at Canada's Drugstore?"

4

This was it, Bentley figured. The perfect chance to redeem herself. "I'll be there in ten minutes! Promise you won't do anything without me!"

But Cal had already hung up.

Uncle Rudy was carefully brushing red dust from his palm into the clay pot when Bentley came back into the dining room. "Sounds like an emergency," he said.

Seeing a ghost probably *was* some kind of emergency, Bentley figured. "I've gotta go, Uncle Rudy, I'll see you later!"

Bentley thought about Cal's ghost, The Dark Man, as she trotted to the garage to get her bike. It made her shiver to think that maybe the man she had seen in the park was the ghost who'd been haunting Cal. She tried to picture the man's face, but she could remember only his faint smile. It wasn't a very nice smile at all.

Bentley pedaled toward Canada's Drugstore at full speed, almost flying the last few blocks up Poplar Avenue to Locust Street. But when she arrived with a flurry and a squeal of brakes, she found Cal leaning casually against the wall of the drugstore, looking nonchalant and almost bored.

"Did I miss him?" Bentley panted. "Where did he go?"

"Geez, Bentley," Cal said, barely moving his lips. "Could you try not to be so obvious?"

"Oh! I get it! Undercover surveillance." She hopped off her bike and tried to act as unconcerned as Cal. It was harder than she thought it would be.

The sunny suburban street seemed perfectly normal, Bentley thought, trying to look around without seeming curious. There was a gray-haired woman waiting for a bus. Two men in suits were coming out of the bank, and another woman was pushing a stroller with a little kid asleep inside.

"He went into the electrical shop across the street," Cal muttered between his teeth.

Electrical shop? What electrical shop? Bentley had lived in Oakfield all her life, but she didn't remember any electrical shop on this street. She let her eyes travel across Canada's big picture window, up to the blue sky, and down again to the other side of the street. There was the red brick bank on the corner of Locust and Poplar and Fran's Four Seasons Hallmark

Shop next door. She knew the Paris Hair Salon that stood next to the card shop. So corny, but comfortable, like the painted pink Eiffel Tower in the middle of the window. Iario's Shoe Repair was next to that. It was a narrow shop all dull green and brown with Mr. Iario always hard at work fixing shoes in the front window.

And, now, there was the electrical shop, right on the alley. The store looked as if it had been there for years. An old wooden sign hung over the sidewalk. It was shaped like a large triangle with an eye and a bolt of lightning painted on it. MORDICUS ELECTRICAL SHOP, the sign said.

How did I miss that? Bentley wondered. It must have been there forever, but somehow she'd never noticed it.

"I think The Dark Man must be Mordicus." Cal's voice was low and husky. "He's a real person who unlocked the store with a key. Would a ghost do that?"

"Are you sure it's the same face?"

Cal hesitated. "Almost," he finally said.

Bentley groaned.

"It's so hard to tell! He shows up in my dreams, but by the next morning I can never really remember him. Sometimes I see him from the corner of my eye, but then he's gone when I look around. I see his reflection for just a second or two in a bowl of cereal or a glass of water and then he disappears! How could I be really sure that I recognize him?" Cal was almost shouting. "That's why I need you to tell me if this is the same man you saw in the park! At least that would be a start! A clue!"

"Okay, okay! Calm down!" Bentley could see why Cal had been acting so odd lately. Being haunted sounded awful!

Cal took a deep breath and spoke quietly and deliberately. "I've got a plan. We go over there together. When we're in the shop—"

"Wait a minute!" Bentley tried to cut him off.

"I'll be right there with you, and all you have to do is look at him. Honest! You don't have to be scared. I'll take care of you."

"It's not that! Just let me think!" Bentley couldn't blame Cal for figuring she was being her usual cowardly self. But she wasn't just afraid. There was something bothering her about this whole thing, something that didn't make sense, and she had to think it through.

Okay, Bentley said to herself, if The Dark Man is a real person named Mordicus who owns an electrical shop, then he can't be a ghost. But how could you explain The Dark Man's face appearing in cereal bowls and dreams and other impossible places? Maybe it was magic, suggested a little voice at the back of Bentley's mind. But she shook her head impatiently at that. Magic was impossible.

Cal was beginning to get restless. "We can just walk in and walk right out," he said persuasively. "Come on!"

"I'm still thinking!" Suppose Mordicus was The Dark Man? He had always stayed out of Cal's sight before. Why did he let Cal see him today? Was it an accident? Or did he want Cal to see him? Maybe it was a trap!

Then Bentley knew there was only one thing she could do to prevent Cal from walking into what might be a trap.

"I'm going alone," she announced.

"No way! If anyone's going alone, it's me! And I'm going now!" Cal started down the street as if he were heading for a showdown.

"Coo-foo-ray!" Bentley yelled.

That stopped him. "Oh, nuts," Cal groaned and turned to face her.

Coup fourré was what you yelled in Mille Bornes when you counterattacked. It was a matter of honor anytime to pay attention to a *coup fourré*. But Bentley had to think fast. If she told Cal this might be a trap, he'd probably want to do something noble like walk straight into it. "It's safer for me if I go alone!" Bentley declared. "The Dark Man knows who you are, so I can't go in with you. It'll look suspicious. I *am* going. So I'd just better go alone!" She wished she felt as brave as she sounded.

"Geez, you're stubborn!" Cal scowled. Then, reluctantly, he said, "Maybe you're right."

"I'll just get a quick look at him and leave!"

"If you're not out in five minutes," Cal said, "I'm coming in after you."

Bentley nodded, hitched her shoulders back, and began the endless walk to the electrical shop.

Her knees were feeling weak and wobbly as she

crossed the street. She walked past the Hallmark store and past Iario's Shoe Repair. Maybe I'll just walk in, Bentley thought. Icy and collected. I'll look Mordicus right in the eye and tell him to leave Cal alone or get out of town. Ha. Fat chance.

Then she was in front of the electrical shop. The shop's name was written in flaking gold letters on its big front window. But the window itself was lined with brown paper so she couldn't see in. Bentley stepped up to the door that was set back from the sidewalk, took a deep breath, and opened it.

The shop was so dim, after the bright sunlight outside, that at first Bentley couldn't see at all. But in a few moments, her eyes adjusted to the half light.

The electrical shop was long and narrow, shaped like a shoe box. Bentley stood at one end looking toward a wooden counter in the shadows at the back of the store. Shelves lined the walls from the ceiling all the way down to the floor. They were filled to overflowing with boxes and piles of junk, all coated with a thick layer of dust. There were twisted wires and odd metal bits, rusty tools, and pieces of old appliances, lamps, engines, and things Bentley couldn't recognize.

The shop smelled of dust, crumbling, yellowed paper, and old varnish. And something more. It was a sharp and spicy scent. Like cloves, Bentley thought. Like electricity. It made the air seem alive. It made Bentley's nose quiver.

"Greetings!" a man's voice called from behind the counter. "Greetings and salutations!"

Bentley took a step forward and then another one. She wanted to turn and run. Take deep breaths, she told herself.

"How may I help you?" the voice said. As Bentley came nearer, a man slowly emerged from behind the counter.

He was tall, dressed in black, with dark hair and a closely trimmed dark beard. But his face was in the shadows. Bentley could see him only as a silhouette against a lamp on the desk behind him.

"Ahoy!" Another voice suddenly called. "Hal-looo!" An enormous bird flew from the shadows at the back of the shop to land on the counter with a flutter of blue-black wings. The bird's nails clicked and scraped on the polished wood, and he tilted his sleek black head at Bentley, regarding her with one shining dark eye.

Bentley stared back, astonished. "I didn't know you could train crows to talk!"

"Crows?" The black bird's voice clattered in his throat. *"Crows?"*

"Klack is a raven," said the man behind the counter. "And very proud of it. Aren't you, Klack?"

"Raven," said the bird. "Mythical prankster. Maker of mischief. Check the legends! That's me." Klack snapped his beak shut with a sound like his name. *Klack.*

It seemed as if Klack understood what they were talking about, Bentley thought. But that was impossible, wasn't it?

"And I," said The Dark Man, "am Mordicus."

Bentley forced herself to take a deep breath and remember why she was here in the first place. She was here to help Cal, and so far, she couldn't tell if Mordicus was the man she had seen in the park. She had to get a better look. She moved toward the counter. "My mom is having something fixed!"

"Oh? And what might this fabulous artifact be?" His voice was deep and silky, and it seemed to Bentley that Mordicus was making fun of her. Mocking. It was a good word for him.

She cast a quick look around. "A clock!" Bentley blurted as she sighted a broken clock face on one of the dusty shelves. "An electric kitchen clock. But I'm not sure I'm in the right place. I mean, maybe you don't have it. Maybe it's someplace else."

"A clock. And the name?" Mordicus pulled a battered metal filebox out from beneath the wooden counter. He opened it and held his hand over a dog-eared collection of cards inside. Klack, the raven, clicked a few steps closer and cocked his dark head to study the box with one bright eye.

Bentley hesitated. She didn't want to give Mordicus her real name. So she gave him the name she always thought she'd like to have. "Fitzhugh," Bentley said. She thought it sounded terribly romantic and impressive.

"Fitzhugh," Mordicus repeated. He bent over the box of cards.

Bentley edged closer, and Klack cocked his head to wink one beady black eye at her. Or at least Bentley thought he did. In this twilight world of dust and darkness, everything seemed confusing and unreal. Bentley was just waiting for Mordicus to look up and tell her he didn't have a clock for a Mrs. Fitzhugh. Then she could get a clear, close look at him and do what every part of her body wanted to do—turn fast and run.

"Ah!" Mordicus plucked a card from the file and raised his head at last. "Here it is!"

"Oh—" Bentley began. Then she looked straight into his eyes.

Suddenly she was lost and falling through an endless darkness.

It seemed as if she had always been there in the darkness. Falling. And always would be. There was nothing else in the universe. Just her. Rushing through empty space.

And then Mordicus must have looked away. Bentley found herself still standing in the dusty electrical shop, holding the edge of the counter with both hands to stay on her feet. "I—" Bentley gasped. "You—"

Klack gave a long, low whistle, ducked his head at her, and twisted around to smooth his wing feathers. "Don't pay any attention to it," the raven muttered and clacked his beak. "Happens to everyone."

"What?" Bentley was thoroughly disoriented. Why was she here? Cal. It had something to do with Cal, didn't it?

Mordicus had half-disappeared into a huge cabinet at the back of the cluttered office behind the counter.

"Got it!" He emerged from the cabinet holding something and smiling.

He *is* the man from the park! Bentley recognized his sly smile. Mordicus. She was willing to bet Mordicus was Cal's Dark Man.

Mordicus came toward her holding something that looked like a cuckoo clock. It was shaped like a house with clock hands on its face.

The little house had a pointed roof that sloped to one side and a round turret with high windows. There was a small picture window at the front of the house and a window like a porthole of blue and green stained glass at the side. A neatly coiled black cord hung from the back of the clock.

"It's yours." Mordicus pressed it toward her. "No charge."

"But—" The last thing in the world Bentley wanted was to take something from the smiling Dark Man.

Mordicus leaned forward, sliding the clock across the counter to her. Klack fluttered and hopped out of the way. "Take it!" Mordicus commanded in a voice hard as a glacier.

Bentley's hands reached automatically to obey. Her skin prickled when she touched the clock. But when she tried to take it, Mordicus held the clock in a firm grip. Bentley froze.

"Little girl." His voice was quiet and dangerous. *"Stay out of things that don't concern you. Stay out of trouble."* Mordicus let go of the clock suddenly, and Bent-

ley stumbled backward, still holding it.

"Oh, for heaven's sakes," Klack muttered. He fluffed his feathers and gave his wings a shake. "Stop bullying the girl!"

Mordicus frowned at the raven, then turned to Bentley with a terrible, cheerful grin. "Have a nice day!"

Bentley walked backward toward the shop door, keeping her eyes on Mordicus. She reached for the cool brass doorknob behind her, eased the door open, and escaped.

After the cool darkness of the shop, Locust Street with all its noise, color, and light seemed like another world. Bentley walked carefully back to Cal, holding the clock as if it were a time bomb. There was something familiar about the little clock house, Bentley thought. She felt as if she'd seen its pointed roof and turret before.

Cal was standing on the curb staring at the clock in her hands as Bentley walked toward him. "That house! It's been in my dreams!"

"It looks familiar to me too," Bentley said. "But not from any dream."

"It was him, wasn't it?" Cal looked up at her. "The Dark Man. The man in the park. And the clock is a message!"

"A message?" Bentley had been so eager to get away from Mordicus that she hadn't stopped to think about what the clock meant. "What kind of message?"

Cal didn't answer. All his attention was on the clock as he reached for it like a knight reaching for the Holy Grail.

"Ow!" Bentley jumped in surprise and pain. The moment Cal's fingers had closed on the clock, an electric shock had seemed to jolt through it. She nursed her aching fingers and scowled at Cal. "Didn't you feel that?"

He was silent. Eyes on the clock, he stood very still, as if he were listening hard to something she couldn't hear.

"Cal!" The electric shock still tingled through Bentley's bones. She rubbed her arms. What was wrong with him?

"Yes." Cal looked blind. Deaf. A million miles away.

"About Mordicus," Bentley said. "There's something wrong." She couldn't find a word for it. He was too tricky. Too pleased with himself. She tried to explain. "I looked into his eyes, and it was like . . . like . . ." She remembered the feeling with a sickening lurch in the pit of her stomach. "Like falling."

"No," Cal said softly. He was looking at the clock and his face glowed with wonder. "It's like flying."

Without another word, Cal marched across Locust Street, back the way Bentley had come.

She hesitated, then followed him. "What are you doing?" Bentley called, trotting to keep up. "Stop!"

Cal ignored her. He walked straight to the door of the Mordicus Electrical Shop, reached for the brass handle, and pulled. But the door refused to open.

There was a sign, Bentley saw, posted on the inside of the glass door. COME BACK LATER!

"It's closed! Let's get out of here."

Cal rubbed his forehead and frowned at the clock. "Then it must be a test." He seemed to be talking to himself.

"You're really making me nervous," Bentley told him.

Cal spun around and trotted off. He cut between the moving cars to cross Locust and hurried back to Canada's Drug with the clock now securely under one arm.

"Am I invisible or something?" Bentley yelled after him. "Have you gone deaf?" She had to run to catch up.

Cal never acted like this! From the moment he had touched the clock, Cal seemed to turn into someone else. Bentley had the odd feeling she was running after some stranger who was beginning to scare her.

5

Half an hour after she left the Mordicus Electrical Shop, Bentley was trudging up the driveway to her house, pushing her bike. The bike had a flat tire. Bentley had gravel stuck in her bloody knees and palms. And Cal had disappeared.

Nobody was home when Bentley let herself in. That was just as well, she decided as she made herself a peanut butter and jelly sandwich. The only thing Bentley really wanted to do right now was to soak in a bathtub filled with warm water and bubbling bath oil.

Soothing, Bentley thought, sinking slowly into the tub. Good word. She sighed. The warm water felt great on her sore knees. I wonder what Cal is doing right now? She couldn't help thinking about him. Probably, she decided, he was hidden away somewhere with that clock.

It was as if somehow the clock had cast a spell over him.

Back at Canada's Drug, he had climbed onto his bike with the clock tucked carefully under one arm.

"Where are we going?" Bentley had asked.

But Cal didn't answer. He just rode away.

Bentley had tried to follow him, shouting his name and pedaling furiously as Cal zigzagged through traffic. But soon he was blocks ahead of her, heading out onto Burlington Street toward the Burlington Mall. Bentley was struggling to keep Cal in sight, riding unsteadily on the narrow, rocky shoulder of the road, when the front tire of her bike suddenly burst. It was like a small explosion that threw the bike into the air and Bentley off the bike. She landed hard and skidded painfully on the sharp rocks.

Sitting in the gravel by the side of the road, she yelled his name once as loud as she could out of pure frustration. But if he heard her, Cal didn't respond.

Mordicus had said to be careful, Bentley remembered as she lay in the warm tub. He said to stay out of it. That sounded to her like a warning. A threat. Was it possible that *he* had somehow made her tire explode?

Anyway, Bentley figured, she was lucky she didn't get thrown in front of a car and flattened. As it was, she was stiff and sore all over with skinned palms, elbows, and knees.

Bentley gingerly picked sharp bits of gravel out of her right knee and watched them sink to the bottom of the tub. Now what? she wondered. She'd have to ask her mom for some money to get her bike fixed and money was always a problem.

Her dad had moved out and gone to California when Bentley was four. A year later, when her parents' divorce was final, he had sent her a postcard with a picture of a palm tree on the front. There was no message written on the card, just a drawing of funny faces. She never heard from him after that. For a long time, Bentley had been mad at her dad. But her mom would never say anything bad about him. She kept explaining that it really wasn't anybody's fault. It was just something that happened. She told Bentley that they could both be sad about it and then get over it. Bentley still got mad or sad if she thought about her dad sometimes. But mostly she just didn't think about him.

He never had sent any money. So her mom had started the first of her businesses. And over the years, she'd started a lot of them.

Maybe her mom would get lucky and sell a Bentley Realty house today. Or maybe she'd sell some other house in the MLS Directory.

The directory! Bentley splashed to attention in the tub making a bubbly tidal wave. The Multiple Listing Service Directory had pictures of nearly every house in town that was for sale, and sometimes Bentley spent hours reading through it and looking at the pictures. Maybe that's where she'd seen the house in Mordicus's clock. That's where she was going to look, as soon as she was done picking gravel out of her knees.

Half an hour later she was in her mom's office, the old den off the front hall, staring at a picture of the house. There was no doubt that it was the same house, and it was only a few blocks away, down by the river on Riverview Drive. Bentley had ridden her bike past it hundreds of times.

According to the listing, the previous owner was called Mr. Murdoch, no first name, and the house was ready for immediate occupancy. Which probably meant it was empty. The realty company listed was Bentley Realty. So her mom must have keys!

Bentley studied the picture in the directory. Cal had been sure the clock was a message. Maybe the message was to go to the Murdoch house. And then what? What did Mordicus want? What was he doing to Cal? The instant Cal touched the clock, he had changed, becoming cold and closed as a steel door without a handle.

It's my fault, Bentley thought. I thought there was some kind of trap and I didn't warn Cal. Then I handed the clock right over to him.

"Anybody home? Help!" her mom yelled from the front hall. "Emergency!"

Bentley jumped up and ran to help.

It was the chicken costume, jammed in the doorway again. Her mom must have been dragging it behind her as she carried in an armload of notebooks and overflowing paper sacks.

Bentley sighed. Her mom should have known it always took two people to get Lydia, the giant chicken, through the front door.

"Take something!" Bentley's mom was about to drop everything while she tugged at the chicken. "Melba's out there attacking the eggs and I've got to rescue them. Oh, and look out for the antipasto, it's leaking!"

"I thought it was a real estate day." Bentley took the notebooks first and set them down on the floor. Then she carefully took the greasy paper bags from her mom. She could hear Melba, their neighbor's small black dog, yapping and growling at the oversized papier-mâché eggs that were strung on a cord to bobble along behind the chicken costume like a line of chicks.

"Lydia was still in the van from last week when I forgot to bring her in." She paused to yell out the door, "MELBA, NO! SHOO!" Then she hurried past Bentley into the kitchen and out the back door, yelling at Melba as she trotted around the outside of the house.

Bentley carried the bags to the kitchen, then went back to the front hall to help her mom get Lydia unstuck. They carried Lydia into the den and left her brooding on her eggs beside the Auto-Ma-Belle.

"Congratulate me," Bentley's mom said. "I sold a house today!"

"Great!" Bentley said. Then her heart started to pound. "It wasn't the Murdoch house, was it?"

"Florentino's. That's why we're eating Italian, in honor of my sale!" Kate Bentley didn't sell many houses. When she did, it was always a special event.

A few minutes later, Bentley was transferring some

leaky olives to a plastic container, holding her nose with one hand so she wouldn't have to smell them, when her mom got suddenly curious. "Hey, why this sudden interest in the Murdoch house?"

"Interest?" One thing Bentley did not want was to get her mom involved. Anyway, what could Bentley tell her that would make any sense?

"No interest in particular," Bentley said. She just wished she could talk to somebody about Cal, the clock, and Mordicus.

That's when Charles called.

Auspicious, Bentley decided. "I want to call a conference," Bentley told him. "You and me."

"Do you want to come over for dinner?"

"I can't. My mom sold a house and we're celebrating. Besides, my uncle Rudy is here."

"Wow! The archaeologist?"

"Anthropologist," Bentley corrected.

"The one who goes all over the world and does all kinds of neat stuff? Can I meet him? Can I come over to your house for dinner?"

Bentley hesitated. "You know my mom can't cook." It was so embarrassing. Especially considering that Charles's mom always made enormous dinners completely from scratch with servings from every food group. Her meals always looked like an illustration from a country farm cookbook.

The last time Charles had come over for dinner, her mom had brought home a bunch of stuff from a health food restaurant. Lentil loaf. Seaweed soup with spongy white bean curd floating around in it.

Mortified. That was how Bentley felt. Of course, Charles thought it was all incredibly funny.

"So what's for dinner tonight?" Charles asked, trying to sound innocent. "Maple pizza?" He was losing control. "Prune and liver casserole?"

Bentley scowled at the telephone. "If you keep laughing like that, you'll probably choke."

Charles struggled to contain himself. "Really, Bentley," he finally said, "can I please come over and have dinner with your uncle Rudy?"

"I have to ask." Bentley checked with her mom and got permission. "You can come," she told Charles and crossed her fingers. She just hoped Italians didn't like prunes and liver. She'd never hear the end of it.

That night during dinner, Charles actually told Uncle Rudy that he was the most fascinating person Charles had ever met. Then he embarrassed Bentley even more by adding, "And probably the skinniest, even though you do eat a lot."

Uncle Rudy laughed so hard he choked on his deli lasagna, and Bentley glared at Charles for being such a dolt. Uncle Rudy couldn't help it if he was skinny.

As they finished dinner, Bentley was getting impatient to pull Charles aside and talk to him alone. But he wasn't cooperating. He was just hanging around the dining room table, practically drooling over Uncle Rudy. And he kept asking questions about the aboriginals and The Rock.

"It's one of the most important Dreaming Places,"

Uncle Rudy told him. "One of the places where the spirits—the Ancestors who shaped the world—returned to the earth, and the aboriginals believe the spirits are still present there."

Charles was listening so hard that he'd been holding his last forkful of lasagna in midair for at least three minutes. It was interesting, all right, but Bentley already knew all this.

"So when they have ceremonies they can speak to the spirits, right, Uncle Rudy?" Bentley was trying to speed things up. And maybe show off a little.

"What kind of ceremonies?" Charles asked.

"Sometimes," Bentley said before Uncle Rudy had a chance to answer, "they'll go to a sacred cave and cut themselves and bleed all over. In some of the caves you can still see bloodstains that soaked into the rocks hundreds of years ago."

"Holy cow!" Charles said.

"It's not as gruesome as it sounds," Uncle Rudy said. "When the elders cut their arms and spill blood, it's a happy event, a kind of celebration."

"Geez," Charles said, "I don't want to know what they do when they're not happy."

"Keep in mind the cultural context," Uncle Rudy said.

"He means everything's different there," Bentley explained. "It's not so weird when you're part of a tribe and everybody thinks it's normal."

"They've managed to survive in a very harsh environment through an incredible closeness to the land," Uncle Rudy said. "And, of course, their universe is magical."

"Magic," Charles repeated.

Magic. There was the word that that small voice in the back of her mind had murmured about Cal and Mordicus and the clock. The idea made Bentley want to wriggle and twist in her chair, as if she had sand in her clothes. "Charles," she snapped, "are you going to leave that fork in the air permanently?"

Charles gave the forkful of cold lasagna a surprised look, as though it had climbed into the air by itself. He put his fork down.

"How about some dessert, Charles?" Bentley's mom asked. "Rudy?"

"It's something from a package," Bentley told Charles. His mom always had homemade cakes and cookies. Maybe he'd skip it and they could go talk.

"Great!" Charles said, and Bentley scowled at him.

"In the outback," Bentley announced, "they eat grubs."

"Holy cow!" Charles turned to Uncle Rudy. "Did you ever eat grubs?"

Bentley's mom moaned. "Rudy, do me a favor and save some of your stories for later. I don't think I can cope with anecdotes about grubs right now, okay?" She stood up to clear the dinner table. Tonight they'd used real china and now they had to wash it all.

"Okay." Uncle Rudy got to his feet too, gathering dishes and silverware to give her a hand. He was halfway out to the kitchen, carrying the salad bowl and a handful of silver, when he stopped and turned to Bentley and Charles. "Pssssst!" he hissed to get their attention. "I did. And they weren't half bad."

Charles's eyes popped in admiration as Uncle Rudy disappeared into the kitchen. Then he jumped to his feet. "Your uncle Rudy is incredible!" He started to gather the last dishes still on the table.

"Listen, I really have to talk to you." Bentley was keeping one eye on the door to the kitchen.

Uncle Rudy appeared in the doorway, talking over his shoulder to her mom right behind him. "Gardner should have been here by now." The gloom and doom look was back on his face.

When they were alone in the kitchen a few moments later, Charles gave Bentley a questioning look. "Gardner?"

"There's some trouble with Uncle Rudy's friend, Dr. Gardner," Bentley explained. "I think that's why Uncle Rudy's here."

"What kind of trouble?" Charles asked.

Suddenly a deep voice seemed to come from out of nowhere to answer him.

"Magic," the voice said. "The trouble is magic."

6

Bentley screamed, Charles shouted, and they both dropped their plates. A few moments later Uncle Rudy and Bentley's mom came running into the kitchen.

"Oh dear," said the voice. "I seem to have put my foot in it."

While everyone else looked around wildly, Uncle Rudy started to laugh. "Gardner! You always did know how to make an entrance!"

"I really am sorry." Dr. Gardner's white hair and beard caught the light outside the open window over the kitchen sink as he moved closer. "I'll just come around, shall I?"

"Right this way!" Uncle Rudy hurried to open the back door and let Dr. Gardner in.

The two men hugged and banged each other heartily on the back, while Bentley, her mom, and Charles stood watching. When they were finally finished, Uncle Rudy introduced his friend all around. Then Dr. Gardner insisted on helping to clean up the mess of broken plates, lasagna, and antipasto on the floor.

They moved to the living room to eat dessert a little while later. It was Lloyd J. Harris frozen apple pie. Not very Italian, but one of Bentley's all-time favorites.

"It was the nicotiana, you see." Dr. Gardner tried to explain why he hadn't come to the front door like most people. "Heady stuff. Fragrance of the night."

"Pardon?" Bentley's mom said.

"Nicotiana. Flowering tobacco," Dr. Gardner said. "It has quite lovely flowers that open in the dark. I followed the scent to your neighbor's garden."

"You were in Mrs. Hudson's garden? In the dark?"

"Best time for it," Dr. Gardner said. "The nicotiana happened to be a wonderfully old-fashioned variety that hasn't been tinkered with to open in the daylight. Unfortunately, the plant breeders have tried to improve things by creating hybrids that bloom all day. But it's humbug. They've only taken the wonder out of it."

"So you were collecting a specimen or something?" Charles asked enthusiastically. After an evening with Uncle Rudy, Charles looked inspired enough to try collecting just about anything.

Dr. Gardner smiled at him. "Enjoying it. Simply enjoying it."

"That's Gardner." Uncle Rudy was grinning. "Always out enjoying things."

Bentley had heard about Dr. Gardner from Uncle Rudy for a long time, but this was the first time she had ever met him in person, and she was studying him carefully.

His thick white hair and short white beard made him look venerable, Bentley thought. And he had deep smile lines around his eyes. His crumpled white suit might have come from some old movie about Morocco, sand dunes, and the foreign legion. There were dirt and grass stains on his knees, Bentley noticed, probably from Mrs. Hudson's garden or some other garden where he'd been smelling flowers.

He looked like a happy person, Bentley thought, and wise as a badger. "You heard us talking about you," Bentley said. "That's why you came to the window."

"You said the trouble was magic," Charles reminded him.

"Ahh," Dr. Gardner said. "Perhaps I'm being unfair to magic. And there are a few more cupcakes involved, I'm afraid."

"Cupcakes?" Bentley repeated.

"Did I say cupcakes?" Dr. Gardner asked. "I meant poodles. No, I mean turnips. Corkscrews." He shook his head. "What time is it?"

Charles checked his watch. "Eight-thirty, exactly. Oh! Make that eight-thirty-one."

"Good. Then it should be over for now. It seems to happen only on the hour and the half hour. And always as regular as clockwork." Dr. Gardner shook his head in puzzlement.

"Saying the wrong word, you mean?" Bentley asked.

"Exactly."

"And you think magic is causing the problem?" Charles asked.

"Oh, no! Magic is an entirely different issue. Of course, this other business does complicate matters."

"But then, what *is* the trouble with magic?" Bentley asked.

"Ah," Dr. Gardner said. "Smoke and fog. It's a matter of rumors."

"It's that backstabber Craven!" Uncle Rudy grimaced and yanked at his hair, making it stand on end. "He's nothing but a jackal. He and his nasty little group are trying to ruin you, Gardner. You must take it seriously!"

"I had thought better of him than all this," Dr. Gardner said sadly.

"Who's Craven?" Bentley asked.

"Craven!" Uncle Rudy thumped his fist on the arm of his chair. "Morley Craven is on the faculty. He's like a viper in the cornfield. A rotten spot at the heart of the fruit, slowly spreading corruption."

Charles gave a low whistle. "He sounds awful!"

"He was a student of mine," Dr. Gardner said. "I had high hopes for him, but poor Morley never really found himself. The problem is, he finds no joy in life."

"The problem is," Uncle Rudy glowered, "good old Dr. Morley Craven wants to be head of the department, no matter what he has to do to get the job."

"I don't understand," Charles said. "What does Dr. Craven have to do with magic? And what are the rumors about?"

Dr. Gardner tugged at his beard. "Here's the problem, Charles—I'm an anthropologist and it's my role to be objective. An observer, not a participant."

"Like a referee," Charles said. "You can't pick favorites."

"Exactly. That also means I can't adopt the beliefs of the people I'm studying."

"Craven has been spreading sly rumors about Gardner's so-called lack of detachment," Uncle Rudy said glumly. "Some people in the department are starting to wonder."

"Maybe you have to be an anthropologist to really understand," Bentley's mom said. "It doesn't sound that bad to me."

"It's like saying he's incompetent," Uncle Rudy explained. "An anthropologist who believes in the magic and legends of the people he studies can't do his job!"

"Character assassination!" Bentley proclaimed.

"Mutiny!" Charles seconded.

Uncle Rudy nodded at both of them. "Exactly. Craven wants to force Gardner to retire. Or he's going to try to get the board of directors to push Gardner out."

"Can he do that?" Bentley looked at Dr. Gardner's

wise, kindly face. It didn't seem possible that some dumb rumors could convince anyone of something bad about Dr. Gardner.

"There *is* the word problem," Dr. Gardner said.

"Oh."

"Maybe it's something physical," Bentley's mom suggested. "Have you been to a doctor?"

"Clean bill of health! The doctors say there's not a thing wrong with me. Of course," Dr. Gardner said cheerfully, "Craven is taking full advantage of it. The latest rumor has it that I'm batty."

Good word, Bentley thought. She tried it out loud to see how it felt. "Batty."

"You mean senile?" Charles asked. "My dad says a lot of people think my grandpa is senile now. But the joke's on them because he was always like that!"

Uncle Rudy turned to blink at Charles with a slow look of wonder on his face, as if Charles had said something pointed and profound. Then he looked at Dr. Gardner, and for a long moment, no one said anything.

"What an idiot I am!" Uncle Rudy said at last. "Gardner, when I was in the bush, hearing the rumors and twisted reports from back here, I have to confess that I began to doubt you. That's why I came back. But of course, you're simply you and Craven is a bag of wind. I should have known better! I'm sorry for ever doubting you!"

"Nothing to be sorry about. I always taught you to check the facts," Dr. Gardner said. "But you're quite right. I am myself. Except on the hour and half hour."

"We'll figure that out, don't you worry!" Uncle Rudy was beaming happily at him. "Everything's going to be fine!"

There would have been a moment of happy silence while everyone smiled at one another, but Bentley's mom always cried easily and she had to blow her nose.

"Well," Charles announced. "I wish I could stay to see what you do at nine o'clock, Dr. Gardner! But I promised I'd be home by then."

"I'll walk you!" Bentley said quickly. She still hadn't gotten a chance to talk to Charles alone.

"You can go," Bentley's mom said. "But be sure to come straight back home!"

Bentley jumped up as Charles got to his feet. But before they left, she walked across the room to offer Dr. Gardner her hand. He stood when she did, polite as an old-fashioned southern gentleman, and his hand, wrapped around hers, was warm and firm.

"I hope I may see you again sometime." Bentley tried to sound formal and refined. Genteel.

"Yeah!" Charles was standing beside her, looking at Uncle Rudy with a goofy, hopeful expression. "I want to hear all about everything!"

Uncle Rudy laughed. "Everything? Then we'll need some time!"

"Great!"

As soon as they were outside, Charles started babbling enthusiastically about anthropology and life in the field and Uncle Rudy, but Bentley was only half-listening. Finally she interrupted him.

"I've got to talk to you," Bentley said. "It's urgent!"

Charles blinked curiously at her, then shrugged. "Okay. As long as we walk while we talk. I'm late."

Charles pushed his bike, and Bentley trotted along beside him. She told him all about Cal being haunted by The Dark Man who turned out to be Mordicus. She told him about seeing Mordicus and Klack, about the electrical shop, the clock, and how Cal left her on Burlington Street when her tire exploded.

As she talked, Charles made companionable noises. He kept saying "Holy cow!" and "Hmmm!" and whistling. But when she finally finished, he was silent.

They walked another half a block through the warm summer night with only the nervous sound of crickets and cicadas breaking the silence. Then Bentley couldn't stand it any longer.

"Well? What do you think?"

They had reached the walk in front of his house, and the porch light lit Charles's round face as he turned to her. "I'd really like to see that talking raven. Can I go with you when you take the clock back?"

"Take the clock back?"

"Well, it's not yours, is it?"

Bentley blinked at him in astonishment. "Charles, you're missing the whole point! Something really weird is going on, and I keep wondering if maybe it could be . . . it could be. . ." Magic, Bentley wanted to say. But it sounded too crazy. And just thinking, *It could be magic,* made her feel hot and cold and gave her a lump in the stomach, all at the same time. It *couldn't* be magic. Could it?

"Everything's got some kind of reasonable explanation," Charles said. "I read someplace that ravens do talk just like mynah birds."

"What about Cal and his dreams? And seeing The Dark Man?"

"I used to have dreams about Santa Claus and King Kong," Charles said. "That doesn't mean they're real. Anyway, guys with beards look a lot alike, and Cal probably just *thinks* this is the same guy."

"Uncle Rudy has a beard and he doesn't look anything like Mordicus!"

"That's different. He's got bright red hair."

"But—"

"Maybe Cal needs to get glasses. Maybe that's why he keeps thinking he sees things that aren't there."

"But you didn't see Cal when he touched that clock. He acted as if he were under some kind of a spell!" There! A spell. Bentley had said it.

Charles shrugged. "Maybe he was just in a rotten mood."

Charles was always so practical! Bentley didn't know what to think.

"I'll tell you what I would do," Charles said. "I'd look in the phone book and see if there really is a Mrs. Fitzhugh. If there is, why don't you call her up and ask her if she left a clock at the electrical shop?"

Bentley stared at him. "How could there be a Mrs. Fitzhugh? I made her up!"

"Co-inky-dinky." In Charles's family, everyone said *co-inky-dinky* instead of coincidence, just like they all said *holy cow*. Bentley used to think it was hereditary and they were born with it.

"But what about Cal?" Bentley asked.

"Call him up. Tell him he's being a crudball and you want the clock back."

Bentley sighed. Charles made it all sound so simple and ordinary.

"Okay," she said. "But what about Mordicus? Who do you think he is?"

"Some guy who fixes clocks."

"But when I looked in his eyes—" She could still remember that terrible lost feeling of falling through space, and she had to shake herself to get rid of it.

"Maybe you had low blood sugar or something," Charles said. "Don't worry so much. Things will work out. Look, I've got to go." He turned and started wheeling his bike away.

"Hey, Charles!" Bentley called softly after him. "Did you ever notice the Mordicus Electrical Shop before?"

Charles looked back at her, blinking thoughtfully. "No." Then he pushed his bike quietly into the shadows.

Bentley ran all the way home, and by the time she came bursting through her front door, she was gasping for breath.

Her mom stuck her head out of her office. "Something wrong, Pip?"

Bentley shook her head.

"You're sure?"

"I'm sure. What happened to Uncle Rudy and Dr. Gardner?"

"They're heading back to the campus. Rudy wants to make sure Craven knows he's in town. Throwing down the gauntlet, he called it. They're going to get ready for a fight."

"Good!" Bentley said. It was important to fight for your friends. Uncle Rudy would fight for Dr. Gardner, and *she* was going to fight for Cal.

"I've got a lot of paperwork to do on this sale," her mom said. "So I'll say good night and pleasant dreams!" She gave Bentley a hearty hug and a loud kiss on the top of her head, then ducked back into her office.

Bentley turned to walk up the stairs. Maybe now, she thought, is the perfect time to call Mrs. Fitzhugh.

7

It had to be a co-inky-dinky, Bentley thought, staring at the listing in the phone book. She was trying not to think about how different it looked from any of the other phone listings.

Fitzgerald Thomas	4012 Essex Ct.	374-6544
Fitzgerald Wm	2344 Clinton Ave.	266-8890
Mrs. Fitzhugh		313-1313
Fitzpatrick D.	315 Linden Ln.	624-7745
Fitzpatrick James	1539 Sunset Ave.	263-8792

But it *was* different. There were just the words *Mrs. Fitzhugh* and the telephone number. It wasn't like the other listings that had first names or initials and addresses. It almost looked as if it had been put there especially for Bentley to find.

Bentley leaned over the page to study the letters, and she caught a hint of a sharp, familiar smell. It was coming from the page in the telephone book, but it wasn't a smell of paper and ink. It was a smell of spice and something else. She leaned closer. Suddenly a spark of static flew from the page up to the tip of her nose and delivered a tiny jolting shock.

Bentley jumped in her chair, and her hand flew to her tingling nose. She watched the telephone book warily as if it were a rattlesnake about to strike. Now she knew why that sharp smell of spice was familiar! It was the smell of the Mordicus Electrical Shop. Somehow Mordicus must have booby-trapped her phone book.

Bentley shivered. But how could he know that she would look up Mrs. Fitzhugh in the telephone book? Maybe he'd been there, listening in the shadows, when Charles suggested it. Or maybe he was in her thoughts the way Cal said Mordicus had come into his dreams. That made her shiver even more.

She leaned a little closer to the phone book, keeping an eye out for sparks. Three thirteens. At least the number would be easy to remember, she thought, trying to cheer herself up. Anytime you wanted to call.

Bentley did not want to call.

But then she thought about how Mordicus seemed to be doing almost anything he wanted, creeping into people's dreams and thoughts and telephone books. And she started to get mad.

Just do it, Bentley ordered herself. How can a phone call hurt you? Ha! she answered herself. If I can get a shock from the telephone book, then I can probably get electrocuted over the phone!

But she took a deep breath, picked up the receiver, and punched in the number.

Instead of a normal ringing tone, Bentley heard the faraway chiming of a musical note. She hung up and tried again. And again the musical note sounded. Maybe it meant the telephone was out of order, Bentley thought. Just to be fair, she decided to try it one more time.

This time, when the note began to sound, Bentley listened more closely, trying to imagine what it could be. It wasn't like any other sound she had heard coming from a telephone, but it did seem familiar. And then she recognized it. It was the sound of a chiming clock.

"Four—five—" Bentley started counting each note. "Eight—nine—" Such a peaceful sound. "Eleven—twelve—thirteen." Then silence.

Bentley suddenly stopped feeling peaceful. A clock that chimed thirteen times! She dropped the receiver back into its cradle and stared at the telephone as if it were a poisoned apple. She had a prickly feeling between her shoulder blades, and she was certain, deep in the pit of her stomach, that something awful had just happened. And this time she was sure it was something magic.

There were just too many odd things happening. Charles's "reasonable explanations" were getting stretched too thin. If you thought about it, only magic really explained everything anyway. Only magic made sense. But most of all, Bentley thought, she could just *feel* the truth of it. She knew, down in the marrow of her bones, that magic was at work.

And right now, it felt as though a trap had clicked shut around her. It was the trap Mordicus had set with his clock.

Bentley jumped to her feet and began to pace. It seemed to her that she'd probably done exactly what Mordicus wanted.

But what could it mean? Bentley pushed her hair off her face and paced faster. What if the clock chiming on the telephone had something to do with the clock that Cal had taken from her?

Bentley checked the time. It was not quite ten o'clock, still early enough to call Cal, and Bentley quickly dialed his number.

He answered before the second ring.

"Cal? It's me."

"Bentley! You have to come over right away and see this!"

"See what?"

"The clock!"

Oh, no, Bentley thought. I *knew* I started something. "Why? What is it doing?"

"You just have to see it," Cal insisted.

"It's late and I'd have to sneak out. And besides, my bike is wrecked." Then she told him about her tire blowing out on Burlington Street while she chased him.

There was silence on the other end of the phone. "I honestly can't remember much about getting the clock," Cal finally said. "But I'm really sorry about whatever I did, especially if you got hurt."

Bentley made a little humming noise. Was this a good time to tell him what she thought? Yes, she decided. "This is going to sound crazy, but I think you might be under a spell."

"A spell?"

Bentley took a deep breath. "Magic. I think Mordicus is using magic."

"Magic! Yes! Of course, it's magic! Bentley, you're a genius! I'm not being haunted at all. It's magic!"

"Well, how do you feel now?" He *sounded* okay, Bentley thought, although she didn't have much experience with this sort of thing. He sounded really happy.

"I don't know if it's a spell or not, but I haven't been able to think about anything except the clock all day," Cal said. "I'll come and get you and ride you over on the back of my bike. I think I've been waiting all my life for this to happen!"

Bentley hung up the phone slowly, trying to think of the perfect word for how Cal sounded. Yearning, that was the word for it, Bentley thought. Maybe everybody yearned sometime for magic to happen to them. But she always thought that magic should be bright and shining. Glorious, that's what magic should be. But this magic from Mordicus seemed sly and cold and dark. So far, it had only made Cal feel haunted and worried. It made him care more about the clock than he did about Bentley, so that he tried to ditch her in town and then left her out on Burlington.

Bentley considered not slipping out to meet Cal. But she couldn't do that. She couldn't desert him to this dark magic when he didn't even seem to see how dangerous it might be.

Bentley crept quietly down the stairs and through the hallway to the kitchen. She let herself out the back door and trotted down the driveway to wait for Cal. She didn't have to wait long. He came speeding like a silver bullet out of the dark, and the moment she climbed on, he took off again at full speed.

Bentley couldn't talk on the way to Cal's house. She had to concentrate on keeping her balance while she teetered on the narrow racing seat of his bike.

When they reached his house, Cal came to a squealing stop, then held the bike while she climbed off stiffly. Her knees still ached where she'd scraped them in the gravel.

Bentley was always impressed by Cal's house. Not only could it have come from some decorating magazine, but it was always absolutely perfectly clean. Dorinda, the maid, kept the place looking as if it was a showcase and no one really lived there. Actually, Bentley thought, no one was there most of the time. Not Cal or his sister or their parents, who were usually at work or traveling or doing something social and sophisticated.

The whole place was done in what her mom would call contemporary decor. Everything was white, gray, or black, and it always made Bentley feel cold. They crossed the enormous living room quickly, headed for Isolation. That's what Cal called the wing of the house set aside for "the children." Cal and his older sister Leanne had their own specially designed section of the house. Cal said it was so that their parents would never have to see them except on special occasions.

Leanne was riding her Lifecycle when Bentley and Cal passed through what Cal's mother, Mrs. Nicholas, called the common room. Leanne was wearing earphones and her eyes were closed, so she didn't even know they were there.

Cal unlocked the door of his room with a small silver key. He opened the door just a crack. "Now, close your eyes," he told Bentley. "And cover them."

With her eyes closed, Bentley heard the door slide open over the plush carpet and felt Cal take her by the shoulders. He steered her into the room and closed the door behind them, then guided her forward as she took small, cautious steps. "Okay," Cal said. "Now you can look."

Bentley slowly moved her hands away from her face and opened her eyes. The room was dark with only a little light seeping under the edge of the door and a glow of moonlight coming through the pleated shades. There was another light in the darkness. It came from the tiny windows of the clock, hanging on the bedroom wall.

"You plugged it in," Bentley said.

Cal pointed. There was the plug, still neatly coiled, hanging free from the bottom of the clock.

"Batteries?"

"No batteries. Keep watching." The light from the tiny windows of the Murdoch house clock lit Cal's face and glittered in his eyes.

Bentley was getting that terrible, tight, scared feeling in her stomach again. Reluctantly, she turned back to watch the clock. Slow seconds went by in the darkness, then a shadow passed in front of the tiny Murdoch picture window, and the downstairs light went out.

A moment later, the light in the turret room grew a little brighter. Then the shadow passed across it. Once. Twice. And back again, as though some tiny figure were pacing the small confines of the turret room.

"It started just before you called," Cal said. "Suddenly the clock chimed and a light went on in the turret room. Then the shadow started moving around the house."

Bentley groaned. "Did it chime thirteen?"

"How did you know?" Even in the dim light, Bentley could see the high, feverish spots of color burning on Cal's cheeks.

"I think I started it." Bentley told him about finding Mrs. Fitzhugh's telephone number, about the smell of spice, the electrical charge from the telephone book, and how she heard the chimes ring over the telephone.

"Fantastic!" Cal was staring at the clock again, gloating like a miser with a golden egg. "And you activated it!"

The shadow in the turret had stopped pacing. It seemed to be standing at the window, looking out at them. Listening.

"Let's give it back," Bentley said.

"What? No way!"

"It's not ours," Bentley argued. "It was . . . ill-gotten. Under false pretenses. It's somebody else's clock."

"No!" Cal had a hungry, desperate look. "Listen, I know you made up the story about the clock in the electric shop just because you had to say something. But I think we were *supposed* to have this clock. It's magic! You said so yourself!"

"Magic." Real magic was a lot scarier than Bentley had ever thought it would be. "What do you think it wants from us?"

"I don't know, but I'm going to find out," Cal said. "First I have to find this house. I'm sure it's a real house, and it's probably right here in town."

"Hmm." Bentley's throat closed tight. Should she tell Cal about the Murdoch house? But suppose she told him the house was probably empty and her mom had the keys? She knew exactly what Cal would want to do. Bentley stared at the light in the tiny turret and the small shadow that seemed to be watching her, daring her to speak. She shivered. "It's late. I want to go home."

Cal didn't seem to hear her. His eyes were fixed on the light in the turret room as the shadow slipped away from the window. Then the light went out and the house was dark. Cal finally turned to her, looking dazed as if he'd been dazzled by a bright light. "We can go now," he said.

He sounded odd, Bentley thought. But she trotted along behind him out of the room.

They didn't talk as they left Cal's house and started the ride back to Bentley's. It seemed to Bentley that the night was much cooler now and the wind was wilder. Most of the houses were dark. People were asleep, and the streets were empty. Cal turned, taking a different route back. He turned again.

"Where are you going?" Bentley said. "This isn't the way to my house!"

Cal leaned into the wind and pedaled harder.

"Hey!" Bentley shouted. Then she had to grab on and hold tight as they swung around a sharp curve onto Riverview Drive. And Bentley realized they were headed straight for the Murdoch house.

8

Cal swerved up a driveway to the sidewalk and squealed to a stop in the darkness between streetlights. Bentley jumped awkwardly off the bike, getting tangled with it and almost falling. Usually Cal helped her, but this time he didn't even seem to know she was there.

He stood staring over an iron fence at a house set back from the street. It was the house with the turret, Bentley saw, the clock house. The Murdoch house. And there, gleaming in the moonlight, was the Bentley Realty sign.

"Cal?" Bentley moved cautiously closer. Cal was so still, he wasn't even blinking. Entranced, Bentley thought. Spellbound. Mordicus must have done this, she decided. He must have guided Cal here somehow. She touched his arm. "Cal?"

He turned and looked at her. "Bentley Realty!" Moonlight gleamed in his eyes as if he were a wolf or some other night hunter. "You can get us in!"

Bentley jumped back. "No!"

"Bentley, I have to go in there! I have to find out what this is all about!"

"Why don't we just forget about this whole thing?"

"I can't forget it!" He looked as if she had told him to forget about breathing. "And I need your help!"

Bentley started walking backward, away from him. She didn't want to look at the house. She didn't want to think about it.

Cal had never asked her for help before. Never. She spun around and walked quickly away, then broke into a jog. "I can't!"

Cal caught up and jogged beside her. "You don't have to go in. Just get the keys for me."

"You mean *steal* them!" It was like some stranger talking. Cal would never steal anything. And he especially wouldn't ask someone else to steal for him. "I won't do it!"

As Bentley ran on, Cal stopped. Was he giving up? Bentley turned to watch him walking back to his bike. "What are you going to do?" she called after him.

Cal answered without turning around. "I'll get in any way I can."

That meant he'd have to break in. Alone. In the middle of the night. Bentley chewed at her lower lip. What if one of the neighbors heard something and called the police? Cal could be in a lot of trouble. Or worse, what if he managed to get inside? What would he find there?

"Wait!" Bentley yelled. "Let's talk about it!"

They talked as Cal walked her home, pushing his bike. The farther they got from the Murdoch house, the more Cal seemed like his old self. More reasonable. More willing to listen. But he was still determined to get inside the Murdoch house and look for a clue to what this "haunting" was all about.

"The dreams, The Dark Man—Mordicus—and that glowing clock are not just going to go away," Cal told Bentley. "I've already been haunted for weeks! All that time, I didn't have any idea what to do about it. Now I've got a clue, and if I don't do something soon I don't know what will happen. It's up to you whether you decide to help me or not. But I have to get into that house."

Bentley was sitting with Cal on the curb outside her house. They sat at the edge of a pool of light from a street lamp. She was chewing the side of her thumb and studying his face in the shifting shadows. His eyes were green and gray as he stared back at her, and the lamplight made his pale hair look white. He looks like a flame, she thought. And it wouldn't be long before he'd be all burned up.

"Okay," Bentley said, still chewing her thumb. "I'll help you."

They'd meet at the Murdoch house tomorrow, they decided. Bentley would get the keys to let them both in. She definitely planned to go along, even though the idea made her stomach feel as wobbly as Jell-O.

No matter how awful she felt, Bentley thought, she just had to do it. How could she live with herself if she let Cal go into the Murdoch house alone?

It was easy to slip the keys out of her mom's office the next morning, but doing it made her feel queasy and sick. Her mom had never actually told her not to touch the Bentley Realty keys. It was just something that was understood, like not robbing a bank or setting the house on fire.

There were two old-fashioned keys. One was large with an ornate head, decorated with silver leaves and fruits and a long shaft. The other was much smaller and plain. They made a heavy weight in the deep pocket of her khaki shorts and bounced against her leg as she walked.

Bentley planned to meet Cal at 9:45 A.M. across the street from the Murdoch house. That was the earliest he could get there after the tennis lesson his parents insisted on. They were trying hard to make Cal perfect.

By 10:06 Cal still hadn't shown up. Bentley was crouched uncomfortably in the bushes on the river side of Riverview Drive, wishing more than anything that she could just leave. She was itchy and hot. Mosquitoes kept buzzing into her ears and leaving bites on the backs of her legs. And, worse, she had the awful feeling that she was about to do something terribly wrong. Something irrevocable. Good word.

Bentley looked out of the bushes onto a bright and sunny street on a perfectly cheerful summer day. Someone was finally coming. But it wasn't Cal. It was Charles, riding his bike with streamers flying, on his way up Riverview Drive.

Bentley ducked back into the bushes, but not soon enough.

"Hey, Bentley!" Charles yelled. He came to a stop in the street in front of her hiding place. "What are you doing?"

"Go away!"

Charles climbed off his bike and wheeled it up to her bush. "Why?"

Bentley heaved a frustrated sigh. "Because Cal and I are going to break into that house across the street and probably both get turned into frogs or something by that guy Mordicus, that's why!"

Charles turned and frowned at the Murdoch house. "It's got a Bentley Realty sign," he said. "Couldn't you get the keys?"

"I've got the keys!"

"Oh," Charles said mildly. "Then it's not breaking in. But what do frogs have to do with it?"

Bentley groaned. "I'm talking about magic!" she said disgustedly. "No matter what you say, I still think we're dealing with magic here. And so does Cal! So frogs are what you get turned into when you get stuck under a magic spell. Right?"

Charles shrugged and smiled. "Like my mom always says, 'To each his own opinion'."

Bentley groaned again. "Go away!"

Charles smiled at her benignly. "Did you try calling Mrs. Fitzhugh?"

"Ha!" Bentley cried from behind her bush. She told him briefly what had happened last night after she left him. He listened and nodded wisely.

"You know," he said, "there's a rational explanation for all of that."

"I don't want to hear it!" Sometimes Charles's practical approach to life was too much to bear.

"Exploring that old house could be fun!" Charles began to drag his bike into the thick brush where Bentley was crouched. "I'll go in with you guys!"

"No!" It was bad enough to feel responsible for delivering the clock and its spell to Cal. And then activating it! She didn't want to feel responsible for Charles too.

"Quit worrying." Charles settled comfortably beside her. "Relax!"

"But—" Bentley began and stopped. Arguing with Charles never did any good. And anyway, Bentley had to admit that having Charles along made her feel safer. She'd wait to see what Cal said. If he ever showed up.

Bentley stared glumly across Riverview Drive at the Murdoch house. "I'm only waiting two more minutes," she announced.

Charles started to hum, looking cheerful as usual, smooth as butterscotch pudding.

"Make that one minute."

"Too late," Charles said. "Here he comes."

Cal was streaking up Riverview Drive, his silver

77

ten-speed and white T-shirt flashing in the sun. He skidded to a stop in front of the Murdoch house.

"Over here!" Charles called, bounding out of the bushes.

Bentley unfolded herself slowly, lagging behind Charles as he trotted out to meet Cal.

"I'm going with you," Charles announced. "Right, Bentley?"

Bentley looked at Cal, expecting him to protest. But Cal only shrugged and headed for the Murdoch house. Charles was just a few steps behind him, but Bentley's feet were lead.

They stopped on the sidewalk, studying the house. It was odd, Bentley thought, how you could go by the old Murdoch house a hundred times on your bike and never really see it. Somehow your eyes would simply slide off.

It was hard to see even now. The house was hidden at the back of a long, narrow lot, screened by overgrown bushes. Vines and dry brush crowded around the house. Spindly trees leaned and rubbed against it.

From where they stood, the house was only an uncertain outline, a pale silver shadow of weathered stucco. Only the pointed roof and the turret could be seen clearly.

"It's small." Charles squinted at the old house. "And kind of beat-up looking."

"Quaint," Bentley said. It was one of her mom's real estate words. "A quaint cottage."

"Most of your mom's houses are like that. Quaint

or eccentric or some other word for weird," Charles said.

Bentley gave him a squint-eyed look.

"I mean," Charles said, "that's one of the things that makes your mom so nice. Somebody has to take care of these weird houses. Somebody sure needs to take care of this one."

The Murdoch house did have a sad, abandoned look, Bentley thought. Orphaned.

A black iron fence surrounded the narrow yard. Its twisted bars of iron were topped with a row of wicked points like thin, sharp spearheads. Cal pushed open the iron gate. "Come on," he said, walking toward the house.

Bentley turned to Charles. "Does the air seem funny to you?" She could swear there was something strange about it. It was like winter, she thought, when you've been scuffing your feet all over the rug and you reach out to touch something, waiting for the shock. The air around the Murdoch house was filled with that feeling of waiting for the sharp crack of electricity.

"You're just worrying again," Charles said. "Let's go." He passed through the gate and up the walk, but Bentley still hesitated.

"Bentley!" Cal called impatiently.

She sighed. How could she back out now with the feeble excuse that she thought the air was humming? She must be imagining it. She passed through the iron gate and hurried to catch up.

The front door of the Murdoch house was made of planks of wood, bound by cross beams and iron studs. It looked like the small side door of a castle, Bentley thought. There was a leaded glass window set in the door like a single eye staring back at them. Overgrown roses and nightshade tangled around the front step where Bentley, Charles, and Cal stood crowded together.

"The key," Cal said.

Bentley reluctantly pulled the keys out of her pocket and gave them to Cal. Then she watched, holding her breath, as Cal fit the old-fashioned key to the lock. But some flicker of movement drew her eyes up to the tiny window—and there she saw a face in the shadows looking out at her.

Bentley screamed and grabbed Cal's arm. "Stop!"

Charles jumped back with one hand clutching his chest. "Holy cow, Bentley! Don't do that! You could kill somebody that way!"

"There was a face!" Bentley saw it for only an instant, but she thought it was the dark, bearded face of Mordicus. She looked again at the window, but now it was shadowed and empty.

"I didn't see anything," Charles said. "Hey! What's the matter with Cal?"

Cal was standing frozen in place, looking blind and dazzled, with his hand still holding the key in midair.

Charles leaned close to peer into Cal's face, and Cal blinked back. "Oh. Nothing serious," Charles declared. "Just a little brain damage."

"Maybe we should get out of here," Bentley said.

"No!" Cal rammed the key into the lock and pushed open the door. "Look! There's nobody here, see?"

He crossed the threshold and marched inside. The dim, quiet cave of the house seemed empty.

"I'm telling you, it's perfectly safe," Cal said from the cool shadows.

Charles turned to Bentley. "Looks okay to me."

Maybe she hadn't seen Mordicus after all, Bentley thought as Charles moved past her into the Murdoch house. Bentley followed, but she stood just inside, looking and listening.

The room was still and shadowy, cool despite the summer heat, and it had the living smell of a forest or a river canyon. A sheet covered the big front window, and the shadows of the trees outside shifted and wavered across it like seaweed moving in the current. It's like being under water, Bentley thought. Green and silent.

One long side of the room held a massive stone fireplace flanked by wooden shelves and cupboards with hooks, crannies, nooks, and tiny doors. In the same wall was a stained glass window, round as a porthole, casting a pool of turquoise and deep purple light onto the wooden floor.

"HALLOO-O-O-O!" Charles yelled, his hands cupped around his mouth like a yodeler.

"Charles!" Bentley shushed him out of reflex. Shouting here was like singing the "Hallelujah Chorus" in the library.

She looked at Cal. Enraptured, she thought. Good

word. "I thought I saw Mordicus looking out at us," she told him. "And if I did, maybe he's here hiding somewhere."

Cal turned to her with his eyes sparkling. Bentley groaned. What an idiot she was! That's exactly what Cal was hoping!

Cal spun around and jogged across the empty room with his sneakers squeaking on the hardwood floor. He disappeared through a doorway to a short hall leading to the back of the house. Charles moved to the fireplace wall and began opening and closing the tiny doors and drawers. Bentley stayed where she was, chewing at her thumb and worrying.

"Cal!" Bentley called. She had a wobble in her voice that made Charles turn and give her a look. He trotted out of sight in the direction Cal had gone.

She heard his shoes grab and squeak across the floor. A pause. Then a door slowly opened. And then there was a terrible strangling noise.

"HA-A-ALLP! HA-LLP!" Charles gurgled. "Killer dustballs!"

"Very funny!" Bentley yelled back, but her heart was jumping like a squirrel in her chest.

Charles appeared in the hall again and grinned at her. "Come on, Bentley," he said. "There's nothing here, just an old empty room. And an ancient kitchen! Archetypal!" That was one of Bentley's favorite words. "It probably has archetypal cockroaches."

Bentley took a deep breath. "Where's Cal?"

Charles looked behind him. "Going upstairs."

An alarm went off in her head. "The turret room!"

9

Bentley raced across the living room, down the hall, and into the kitchen. A steep stairway led from the kitchen to the second floor, and Bentley ran up it with Charles at her heels. They almost collided with Cal who was standing in the narrow hallway.

"I don't understand!" He looked disappointed and puzzled. "There's no sign of Mordicus, and the turret room is empty."

"Good!" Bentley said. "Then we can leave!"

"Oh, come on, Bentley," Charles said. "As long as we're here, we might as well look around!"

Bentley had to admit, she *was* curious about the old house. "You're sure there's no sign of him?"

Cal shook his head. Sorrowful, Bentley thought.

"I guess it won't hurt," she said.

"Yeah!" Charles's face lit up. "An adventure!"

They spent over an hour exploring the old house.

Charles was certain they'd find a skeleton in the basement, and they searched everywhere for secret panels and passages. But all they found was dust.

The two best rooms, they agreed, were upstairs. One was formed by the point of the steep slope of roof, and only Charles, who was the shortest, could stand fully upright in the highest part of the room. A window looked from the end of the room across the long front yard to Riverview Drive and the woods and river beyond. From here, Bentley could see where she and Charles had hidden and waited for Cal.

The view from the turret was entirely different. That's where they stood now, taking one last look around before they left. There were three windows set into the curving wall. Each looked out into the heart of the treetops, and the light that filtered through the trees gave the room a cool green glow. An ornate curio cabinet was built into one side of the turret room. Glass-paneled doors guarded empty shelves. And in the middle of the cabinet were two square wooden doors. As she looked closely, Bentley could see that each tiny handle on the wooden doors was carved in the shape of a cat's head.

Cats! I get it, Bentley thought. It's a joke! Everybody knows cats are curious. And these are curious cats on a curio cabinet. She stroked one of the cat heads lightly, then tugged at the handle.

But curiosity killed the cat.

Bentley remembered the saying with a start, and her hand leapt off the handle. She frowned.

There was probably some other perfectly good

saying about curiosity being useful. She'd have to remember to ask her mom. As for right here and now, Bentley refused to be scared off by a cabinet.

She used both hands to tug at the wooden doors. But, though they rattled and shook, the doors wouldn't open.

Cal was soon standing beside her, studying the locked doors. He reached out with one finger and gently touched a small keyhole set beneath one of the handles.

"The other key!" he suddenly cried. "The little key that came with the house key!" He began to search his pockets for the keys to the Murdoch house, but he had given them back to Bentley. "Bentley! Use the key! Open it!"

"Yeah!" Charles stood on her other side. "Who knows what we could find in there! A treasure map or a fortune in jewels!" Bentley reluctantly drew the keys from the pocket of her shorts and carefully slid the smaller silver key into the lock. It was a perfect fit. The key turned with a soft click, and Bentley pulled the cabinet door open.

The interior of the cabinet was deep and dark, and at first Bentley didn't see a thing. But Charles did.

"A book!" He snatched the book from the shadowy cabinet an instant before Cal could reach it.

The book in Charles's hands was covered in deep red leather. Its name and the name of the author were printed in gold. *"Between the Cracks,"* Charles read aloud, "by Dakin."

He examined the front and back covers, then tried

to open the book. But it seemed as solid as a block of wood.

"It's a fake!" Charles announced. "A fake book!"

"Let me see." Bentley took the book from Charles and tried to pry the covers apart. No luck.

Then Cal took the book. He ran his hand lightly over the gold lettering on the deep red leather and, without effort, in one smooth motion, lifted the front cover. There was a sharp smell of spice as the book opened, and, for just a moment, a soft glow from inside the book seemed to light Cal's face. He turned a page. Then he turned another and another with a look of delight.

"How did you do that?" Charles was completely dumbfounded.

Magic. That was the only answer. It had to be magic, Bentley thought with a sinking feeling. She looked over Cal's shoulder at the blank white pages of the book and then at Cal's face. Why did he seem so pleased?

Charles craned to look at the empty pages. "Nuts! There's nothing in there."

"What?" Cal frowned.

"Blank. Nothing there."

"But it's crammed with tiny, old-fashioned hand-writing and lots of little drawings!" Cal tore his gaze away from the little book to look at them.

"Oh, sure," Charles said. "Invisible writing."

Cal looked from Charles to Bentley.

She shook her head. "I don't see anything."

Cal looked at the book in his hands with growing

wonder. "Then it must be meant just for me!" He clapped the book shut and ran out of the room. They could hear him race down the stairs.

"Hey, Cal!" Charles called after him, trotting to the door of the turret room.

Bentley saved her breath.

"I don't get it." Charles shook his head, coming back to her. "If Cal saw some writing in that book, why wouldn't he tell us what it said?"

Bentley sighed. "I'm beginning to think magic makes people selfish and mean. *This* magic, anyway." She looked around the green shadowed room, feeling as if Mordicus had been there all along. Right now he'd be laughing at her again. "Let's get out of here."

As they were leaving, Bentley carefully locked the heavy front door of the Murdoch house. She wished she'd never opened it.

"You know what this reminds me of?" Ever since they left the turret room, Charles had been talking nonstop about magic. "It reminds me of *The Once and Future King!* Remember the Sword in the Stone that turned out to be Excalibur and only the rightful king of England could pull it out? Doesn't that remind you of Cal and that red book? Like he was chosen for something?"

Bentley looked around her at the old Murdoch house and its neglected garden. Bleak. Forlorn. "The question is," she said glumly, "chosen for what?"

10

Bentley walked part of the way home from the Mur-doch house with Charles. He was pushing his bike and chattering about Cal and the mysterious book while Bentley listened gloomily. She couldn't get a word in to remind Charles of how this sly magic was affecting Cal. Or how she was afraid it might mean they'd eventually lose Cal as a friend. Look at how he'd changed already! First he'd deserted her on Bur-lington Street, and now he'd dumped her and Charles both.

Charles talked all the way to the corner of Keeney and Colter where they said good-bye and went in separate directions. He jumped on his bike and rode away, noisily honking his bike horns. Bentley waved, then turned and started toward home.

Things kept on getting worse and worse, she thought. Not only was Cal acting like some selfish stranger and going off alone to hide, but now even Charles was leaving. The Donovans were going away for a few days to visit relatives. She was on her own.

Maybe Cal was still under some kind of spell, Bentley thought as she trudged along, and that's why he didn't seem to care about her and Charles anymore. Or maybe he wasn't under a spell. Maybe now that he'd found magic, he decided he didn't need friends anymore. Nuts, Bentley thought. I still want to be friends with Cal. And I want him back the way he used to be.

When she got home Bentley was glad to see Uncle Rudy sitting at the kitchen table drinking something peachy-pink. He had pink foam in his red beard, and Bentley gave his glass a questioning look.

"It's a Strawberry Sunrise." Uncle Rudy waved the glass at her. "Want some?"

"What's in it?" You had to be careful with Uncle Rudy. He was worse than her mom about eating strange foods. He'd eat almost anything.

"A de-luscious blend of strawberries, orange juice, and frozen yogurt. Taste it."

Bentley took a cautious sip from his glass. "It's good."

"Aha! A customer!" Uncle Rudy jumped to his feet and started bustling around the kitchen. He seemed much happier now than when he first arrived.

"How is Dr. Gardner doing with his word problem?" Bentley sat down at the table and turned her chair so that she could watch Uncle Rudy.

He crinkled his face. "Still ferhoodled on the hour

and half hour." He winked at her. "Ferhoodled, you might like to know, is Pennsylvania Dutch for mixed-up and confused."

"Ferhoodled." Bentley tested the word and nodded. "I like that. But haven't you figured out yet why it happens?" On the hour and half hour. Like clockwork, Dr. Gardner had said. Then Bentley scowled. Clocks again. That reminded her of Mordicus and she didn't want to think about him.

Uncle Rudy shook his head. "No clues yet."

"You admire Dr. Gardner a lot, don't you?"

"Absolutely. Gardner's a fine teacher and a brilliant anthropologist."

"And he's your friend too, right?"

"Right!" Uncle Rudy was busily slicing strawberries and tossing them into the blender.

"What if you thought he was making a big mistake?" Bentley asked carefully. "And you thought he was doing something stupid, but he didn't know it was stupid? And besides that, he hurt your feelings."

Uncle Rudy stopped dropping strawberries into the blender to regard her thoughtfully. "Are we still talking about Gardner and me? Or are we maybe talking about you and a friend of yours?"

"Oh," Bentley said, "I'm just talking about friends in general."

Uncle Rudy tugged at his beard. "I see. Then, in general, I'd say that if you think a friend is making a big mistake, you owe it to your friend to tell him or her what you think and try to help, even if you did get your feelings hurt. Somebody in trouble might hurt other people without meaning to. They get so wrapped up in the trouble or in themselves that they just don't notice."

"Hmm." That sure sounded like Cal, Bentley thought. "So it's up to you to stay loyal and stead-fast."

"Yup." Uncle Rudy spooned in frozen vanilla yo-gurt, added a splash of orange juice, and turned on the blender. In a few seconds he had a pitcher of thick, fresh Strawberry Sunrise. He poured Bentley a full pink glass with a flourish and a bow, then joined her at the table. They both raised their glasses in a salute and drank deeply.

Uncle Rudy wiped pink foam from his mustache and looked at her very seriously. "Listen, Pip, you know if there's anything you want to talk about, you can talk to me. Remember, I've got big ears."

Bentley was stuck. This could be the perfect time to tell Uncle Rudy about Cal, Mordicus, the clock, and all of it. But she'd have to tell him about how she took her mom's keys, and she felt awful about that. Her mom always trusted her, and Bentley had taken advantage of it. And Uncle Rudy probably wouldn't believe that Mordicus, the raven, the clock, and the book were really magic. Unless he saw it all for him-self, and that would mean taking Uncle Rudy to see Cal.

But it would be like betraying Cal to get Uncle Rudy involved. She would be telling him Cal's secret. Cal had been haunted for weeks before he told *her* about it, and he didn't even know Uncle Rudy.

Then suppose she did convince Uncle Rudy that magic was involved? Anthropologists weren't supposed to believe in magic—Uncle Rudy said so himself.

She took a slow sip of her Strawberry Sunrise. "I'll remember, Uncle Rudy." Then she grinned at him. "Anyway, your ears aren't so big! Maybe you should just comb your hair down over them!"

Uncle Rudy clapped both hands over his ears. "Ha!"

Bentley laughed, then got serious. "What's Dr. Gardner going to do?"

Uncle Rudy made a wry face. "My coming back from the bush has suddenly gotten things rolling. Gardner has realized that this business with Craven is really serious. So, being Gardner, he wants to take action immediately. He's decided to call for a formal hearing between the dean and the entire anthropology department as a way of getting any questions about his competence out in the open."

It sounded like a trial, Bentley thought. It sounded scary. "You're going to stick up for Dr. Gardner, aren't you?"

"Of course." Uncle Rudy grinned. "Steadfastly. And somehow we'll figure out a way for Gardner to avoid talking or doing much of anything at the hour and the half hour, so he doesn't get ferhoodled." He ran his fingers through his red hair. As usual, it was standing on end. "But enough of that! How about some food to go with these drinks? I'm starving!"

Bentley realized she was hungry too, and they

rummaged and poked through all the cabinets and the refrigerator, looking for interesting things to eat. Foraging, Uncle Rudy called it. They finally put together a lunch buffet of leftover lasagna, leftover Chinese, some frozen cheese Danish, a hunk of cheddar, and a jar of hot Italian peppers. Most of it was Uncle Rudy's idea.

As they made lunch, Bentley told him about Charles's huge family, the Donovans. She was still getting warmed up on the subject when they sat down to eat. "It's all very democratic. They have family meetings and everything." To Bentley it sounded like something only families on TV did.

Bentley was having a hot-pepper-and-cheddar-cheese-on-a-Danish-Uncle-Rudy-Special with a huge side dish of cold Three Delicacies Delight. She had a mouth full of food when Uncle Rudy asked her a question.

"How's the other friend you wrote me about? Cal?"

"Mmm." Chewing heartily, Bentley pointed at her bulging cheeks, then held up a finger asking Uncle Rudy to wait for an answer. But what could she say?

She swallowed hard and shrugged. "Okay," she said with her mouth still half full of food. But Cal wasn't okay. And Bentley suddenly decided she'd spent long enough moping around. It was time to do something. She swallowed again and washed it down with Strawberry Sunrise. "I think I'm done now."

Uncle Rudy raised an eyebrow at her half-eaten sandwich. "Too much hot pepper?"

"No, it was perfect." Bentley stood up and carried

her plate to the counter to wrap it in Handi-Wrap. "I just wasn't that hungry. And there's something I have to do."

She was going to see Mordicus, Bentley decided. Going alone to the electrical shop for a showdown.

Deciding to do something brave and heroic was easy when you were in your own kitchen, Bentley thought as she peered out the window of Canada's Drugstore. Actually doing it was a lot harder.

She had been hovering near the paperback book rack in Canada's big front window for almost twenty minutes. From here she had a clear view of the Mordicus Electrical Shop. When she first arrived, Bentley thought she'd take only a few minutes to look over the electrical shop and see if anything looked suspicious. But now she was having a terrible time persuading herself to move on.

Where's your courage? she scolded herself. Coward! A truly worthwhile person should have determination. Pluck. Grit. Great words, she thought. But not inspiring enough to make her leave the safety of Canada's, cross the street, and march into the electrical shop. Then she saw Cal.

He came flying up Locust Street on his silver bike, crouched over the handlebars, all speed and elbows with the sun glaring off his white T-shirt and white-blond hair. As he squealed to a stop under the sign of lightning and the painted eye, Bentley was out the door of Canada's Drug, running up Locust after him without thinking at all.

Cal had barely passed through the door of Mordicus's shop when Bentley threw it open behind him. She stood blinking in the familiar dusty gloom while Cal, halfway up the length of the shop, turned to scowl at her.

"Bentley! What are you doing here?"

Bentley drew herself up. Pluck, she reminded herself. Determination. And steadfast loyalty. "I want to talk to Mordicus."

"Is there a problem with your clock, Miss Fitzhugh?" said The Dark Man standing behind the counter at the back of the shop. His smooth voice had a mocking edge.

Bentley could feel herself blushing. "My name isn't Fitzhugh. It's Bentley. And I don't have your clock anymore." She moved forward with her heart pounding. "Cal does."

Klack, the raven, landed on the counter with a flutter of blue-black wings. "Of course he does," the raven said in his harsh and raspy voice. "And the book too, as Mordicus well knows."

Mordicus frowned at the black bird. "I was just having a little fun, Klack. Why be so serious?"

"It *is* serious." Bentley took a deep breath and walked to Mordicus. "You've been haunting Cal, and you've been using me to make things worse and worse. First the clock and then that book in the Murdoch house! I've got a right to know what you're doing and why!"

"If anybody has a right to know what's going on," said Cal, stepping up briskly beside her, "it's me! And Bentley, you don't need to be here at all!"

"Ha!" Bentley glared at him.

Mordicus chuckled. "That's what I like to see! True friendship in action. And haven't I always said, Klack, that true friendship is something very rare? In fact," The Dark Man's voice and face grew cool as a stone, "one doesn't see it at all."

Klack paused in preening his long wing feathers. "What you see often depends on what you look for."

That was something her mom might have said, Bentley thought. Mordicus probably would look for the worst in people. He didn't seem to like people very much. But Bentley was beginning to think the raven was on her side. Just then the bird cocked his dark head and winked one beady black eye at her.

Mordicus coughed once for attention and concentrated his dark gaze on Cal. "What I want is simple. It's you."

Bentley shuddered. "What do you mean?"

But Mordicus and Cal both ignored her. They were staring at each other, eyes locked together. "I've been calling on you regularly for nine weeks past," Mordicus told Cal. "I've been a face that passed over the moon, a shadow at the corner of your eye, a word in a book you've been reading. I've been that annoying itch on the bottom of your left foot. I've been a pricking of your thumbs, a vague longing, the sharp cry of a bird at midnight."

Bentley glared at The Dark Man. "You don't have the right to do that! Nobody has the right to haunt and hound someone the way you've been haunting Cal!"

"Ah!" Mordicus turned toward her. He looked amused and pleased with himself. "Who's talking about rights? I'm talking about power. That's my real business. Power. If you've got it, use it. As my old teacher, Dakin, used to say, 'If you see something you want, take it'."

"He never said anything of the sort!" Klack said crossly.

"How would you know?" Mordicus snapped at the bird. "Dakin disappeared two hundred years before your time!"

"I know what I know." Klack snapped his beak shut.

"But *why* were you haunting me?" Cal demanded. "What do you want?"

"I'll make it plain," Mordicus said. "I'm in the market for an apprentice, and you've caught my eye. I want you to listen and learn, to help with spells and clocks and things."

"No!" Bentley's stomach clutched. Mordicus was spoiled. Blighted. And he would spoil everything around him.

But Cal's face was turned to Mordicus like a sunflower to the sun. As if he were entranced, Bentley thought. Enchanted. She grabbed his arm and yanked on it hard. "Don't do it!"

Cal didn't even look at her. "Cut it out, Bentley," he said mildly.

"Oh, yes. Bentley." Mordicus turned to her with a sly smile. "Now, what shall we do with you?"

11

Three days later, Bentley was on her way home from the bike repair shop when she saw Charles in the park with his little brother, James Francis. She rode over to join them.

"We just got back this afternoon," Charles said. "So what's new? Anything been happening?"

Bentley frowned a little and shrugged. The headache she'd had on and off for days had suddenly flared up again. "Nothing."

"You got your bike fixed fast."

Fast? Bentley couldn't quite remember what had been wrong with her bike in the first place. Her head throbbed harder.

"Hey!" James Francis yelled. He was running in joyful circles in the late afternoon sunlight, arms held straight out at his sides and a beatific smile on his face.

"Hey," Bentley called back.

Charles shook his head. "Sometimes I think he's a lot like a dog. You know how dogs run in circles when they're excited?"

They watched James Francis fall on his face in the grass, pop up onto his elbows with a grin, then clamber to his feet to start running again. Sooner or later, Charles told Bentley, James Francis would wear himself out enough to go home without a fuss.

"How long can he keep doing that?" Bentley asked.

"He's almost done," Charles told her. "He'll fall one or two more times and then just lay there. Then I can take him home for dinner."

"Can I come with you? My mom has to work tonight, and Uncle Rudy is out with Dr. Gardner." Bentley's mom would be a giant walking tennis ball at a tennis tournament tonight. She had ball costumes for almost every sport, from football to basketball to golf.

"Sure," Charles said. "My folks won't mind. What's your Uncle Rudy doing with Dr. Gardner? Is Dr. Gardner still batty?"

"Ferhoodled—that means mixed-up—and just at the hour and half hour." Like clockwork. A lightning bolt of pain shot through Bentley's head.

"And what about Cal?" Charles asked. "What's happening with him? Has he told you what's in the book?"

The pain was so bad now that she could barely see, and her own voice seemed to be coming from far away. "Cal?" Something sad had happened, Bentley thought, but she didn't know what. When she tried to concentrate, her thoughts would simply skid away as though the thought were slipping off some smooth, slick wall in her mind. And then there was the headache. It was so bad now, she could barely think at all.

"What did Cal do with the book? What's it all about?" Charles frowned, frustrated and impatient.

But Bentley couldn't make sense out of what he was saying while her head pounded and throbbed. He seemed to be talking from the end of a long tunnel, and it made her queasy, as though she were seasick. Or falling.

"James Francis hit the dirt." Bentley's voice was a faint croak. She concentrated on the two-year-old lying in the grass, and the pain in her head eased. "I think he's going to stay down this time."

"COCOA!" James Francis yelled. But his voice was muffled because his face was buried in the grass. He sat up. "COCOA!!"

Charles scowled at Bentley a moment longer, then shook his head and trotted over to James Francis.

"Cocoa is in the wintertime." Charles hoisted his little brother to his feet. "This is summer."

"Cocoa," James Francis insisted.

"You can ask Mom." Charles had James Francis by the hand and started walking him toward home.

Bentley watched them go, feeling like a castaway marooned on a desert island as a rescue ship steamed away from her.

"Oh, come on, Bentley!" Charles shouted over his shoulder. "I'm starving!"

Having dinner with the Donovan family was better than a vitamin. There was laughter and noise and a feeling of belonging that was as comforting as her favorite bathrobe.

The first time Bentley ate dinner with the Donovans was back in third grade when she and Charles had met. Charles always said Bentley just followed him home from school one day, but Bentley insisted he must have invited her. That was the year she was new in school and Charles adopted her. He was always adopting something, like that squirrel without a tail he fed all last winter.

It seemed as if all the Donovans were always feeding something or somebody, and it was just natural for Bentley to be eating lunch or dinner there at least once a week.

Bentley especially loved the time just before dinner when everyone was jostling and swooping around the kitchen, getting the meal ready, all talking at once.

They all really like each other, Bentley thought. You can tell, even though they make faces and groan and sometimes argue.

Natalie was the oldest. In the fall, she'd be a senior in high school. Natalie could always get everybody organized without being bossy. Charles's other sister, Eileen, was going to be a sophomore, and according to Charles, she spent more time on the telephone than the rest of the family put together.

"Tell Sean you'll call him back," Natalie said now as she handed Eileen a big metal strainer for the green beans.

Eileen made a face, but got off the phone quickly. "That was *Brian* I was talking to!" she announced. "And for everybody's information, I'm not ever speaking to Sean again."

"Oh!" The Smudge, who was a year and a half older than Charles, dramatically clapped his hands to his chest. "Sean bites the dust!" He made loud grunting, dying noises while the boys laughed and the girls groaned.

Of the boys, Arthur was the oldest, and after Charles, he was Bentley's favorite Donovan. A very congenial person, she thought. Simpatico. Good word.

Charles said Arthur was going through a "growth spurt." Meaning most of his clothes were too small and he seemed uncomfortable a lot of the time. But at the moment, Arthur was very deftly making mashed potatoes, and Bentley watched as he judiciously added lumps of butter and splashes of milk.

Charles dashed past with plates and silver. "Grab some napkins, will ya, Bentley?"

Bentley had to maneuver around Natalie, who was stacking hot, oven-fried chicken onto a giant-sized platter, and step over James Francis. He was clanging steadily on the stove with his battered old wooden spoon as Arthur turned on the electric mixer. The Smudge decided to add to the noise and began to sing at the top of his voice. "Home, home on the range, where the deer and the cantaloupe play. . . ."

"Holy cow! This is some rowdy group!" Mrs. Donovan exclaimed as she came flying into the noisy kitchen.

"Music!" James Francis yelled.

"Dinner!" Mrs. Donovan yelled back. "Let's eat!"

Bentley's regular seat was near Mr. Donovan and Natalie at the quieter end of the table. That was fine with her, because James Francis was still in the food-throwing stage. Charles was on her left and Arthur sat across from her.

"Charles has been telling us about your uncle Rudy," Mr. Donovan said as he passed her the chicken.

"Yeah, Charles thinks your uncle Rudy is a cross between a superhero and Albert Einstein," The Smudge said.

"Dr. Gardner's more like Albert Einstein," Charles said with his mouth full of green beans. "He's got white hair that sticks up all over his head."

"He's brilliant," Bentley added. Wild hair only made Dr. Gardner sound messy. "He has a very illustrious reputation."

"Distinguished. Well-known in his field," Mr. Donovan translated. He looked at Bentley with a gleam in his eye. "How would you like to see our new car? I'd like to know what adjectives you'd put on *it*."

"Just new to us," Mrs. Donovan said from the other end of the table. "Actually it's more of a relic."

"A classic, Mom," Arthur said firmly.

"Arthur, why don't you and Charles take Bentley out to look it over after dinner?" Mr. Donovan turned to Bentley. "All right with you?"

"Sure." Bentley shrugged.

Dessert was homemade chocolate cake with chocolate icing, and Bentley stuffed herself. It was such a relief to eat normal food sometimes.

From the moment she saw the old car, Bentley couldn't take her eyes off it. She stood with Arthur and Charles in the Donovans' driveway and just gawked.

"It's a 1949 Mercury sedan," Arthur explained. The old car was enormous. Forest green, rounded, and curving and graceful as a bumblebee.

"There's a bird on its nose!" Bentley said. It was a streamlined bird with flowing wings, waiting for the wind. "Can I touch it?" She was already trailing her hand softly over the bulge of the fender. "There's a spear!"

A thin silver spear ran along the length of the car. Bentley studied the Mercury from a new angle. It was a wise old turtle of a car. Nothing bad could ever happen to you in it, Bentley thought.

"There's maybe ten thousand of the '49 Mercs left," Arthur said. "And only about two hundred of them are in original condition, like this one. Most of them got stripped and painted with flames and stuff by hot-rodders."

"They're an endangered species," Charles said. "Like whales."

Bentley walked around to the back of the car. "There's a face. It's Mercury!" She recognized the old Greek god by the winged helmet he wore, the symbol of speed. His face was a tiny raised silver sculpture in the ornate emblem where the key to the trunk would fit.

"He's everywhere," Charles told her. "Check out the steering wheel."

Arthur opened the driver's door, and Bentley leaned into the quiet cave that was the interior of the car. In the center of the steering wheel was another portrait of Mercury in his helmet. Bentley inhaled the smell of soft leather and polish. Just being inside the car was like traveling in time. "It's wonderful."

"I wonder what Cal would think of it." Charles was watching her carefully.

A sharp pain struck her head, and Bentley backed out of the car. "Cal?"

"Hey, Bentley, are you okay?" It was Arthur, so far away that Bentley could hardly hear him. She put a hand on the cool roof of the old car. "Cal. The clock."

"Is she going to faint?" someone asked. That was the last thing Bentley remembered.

12

Charles was really impressed. "Wow!" he kept saying. "I've never seen anybody actually faint!"

Bentley was sitting up now on a grassy stretch next to the Donovans' driveway. There was a dull, steady throbbing in her head, and she felt hot and dizzy. Charles and Arthur sat on either side of her. Arthur was watching her with a worried look, but Charles acted as if she had accomplished some neat trick.

"You just melted like Jell-O! It's a good thing Arthur caught you before you hit the driveway."

Bentley scowled at him. She didn't want to talk or think about fainting anymore.

"How do you feel?" Arthur asked. "Are you sick?"

Bentley shook her head. "I'm okay. I just want to go home."

"I'll tell my dad and he can drive you home or maybe to a doctor." Arthur stood and offered a hand to pull her up.

"No!" Bentley jumped to her feet. "I'm all right!"

"Yeah, except when somebody mentions Cal." Charles gave her a sideways look from his seat on the grass. "Have you noticed that?"

Bentley couldn't answer. The pain was stabbing at her, wiping out all thoughts. "I have to go home!" She turned and ran for her bike parked at the front of the house.

"Hey!" Charles yelled after her.

Bentley kept running. All she wanted to do was get home to the safety of her own room.

She must have fallen asleep for a while, Bentley thought. It was dark outside. She was lying on her bed with the lights still on, and the book she'd been reading was open beside her. But something had woken her up.

Bentley lay still, listening to the quiet house. Probably nobody else was home yet, she decided. It must have been just some noise outside. Then she noticed the feather.

It was a large black feather falling very, very slowly, drifting through midair in the center of her room, coming from nowhere in particular. Bentley watched it float dreamily downward and propped herself up on one elbow to see it land on the rag rug next to her bed. The black feather had settled beside a book covered in deep red leather with gold script on its cover.

She swung onto her feet and bent cautiously toward the book to read the title. *Between the Cracks,* it said. *By Dakin.* Something rang in her memory like a sluggish warning bell going off, but Bentley didn't stop to think. She picked up the book.

The leather binding felt cool and smooth in her hand and somehow familiar. A small, downy feather marked a place in the book, and it seemed only natural to see what was inside.

As Bentley opened the book, all her memory came rushing back. She remembered Cal's haunting and the clock and Mordicus and the shop and the Murdoch house. Suddenly her head wasn't throbbing anymore and the slick wall in her mind was gone.

She looked with amazement at the book in her hands. It was the same book Cal had taken from the Murdoch house! But what was it doing here? And how had she been able to open it?

Maybe the downy feather marking a place in the book had made it possible. Bentley looked thoughtfully at the long black feather lying on her rag rug. The feather was as black as the raven in the electrical shop. She looked around her empty room and said the raven's name out loud. "Klack?"

There was a flutter of feathers and the familiar click of claws on wood.

"Well done! An excellent deduction." Klack was standing on Bentley's desk, head cocked toward her with one bright, black eye shining approval.

Bentley's heart started to pound. He wasn't there a moment ago, she was sure of it!

"You have a logical mind," the raven said in his raspy voice. "And some talent in the way of intuition. A good combination." Klack hopped onto the back of her desk chair. "Well? What does your intuition tell you?"

Bentley drew a deep breath and contemplated the raven. "I think you want to help me," she said. "But I don't know why."

"I have my reasons. Besides, ravens are all meddlers, it's part of our nature. A little mischief, a little meddling between Mordicus and your friend Cal is just my cup of tea." Klack smoothed his wing feathers thoughtfully. "Mordicus isn't such a bad fellow, you know."

"Ha!"

"It's all the power," Klack said. "He hasn't handled it well. And neither has your friend, has he?"

Bentley was going to protest that Mordicus must have put a spell on Cal. But she knew better. It was Cal himself who had been acting mean and selfish. She nodded slowly.

"Too much power," Klack said. "And besides, Mordicus is lonely."

"Wait a minute, are you trying to make me feel sorry for him?" She wouldn't do that! Mordicus was still as much of a bully as Todd Lunden. Worse! Mordicus hadn't only given her a headache, he'd tried to steal her friendship with Cal. For days now she hadn't even been able to think of Cal without that throbbing pain. Anyway, maybe Cal had been acting like a crudball lately, but she didn't believe he would ever be as mean as Mordicus.

"It's just a truth to keep in mind," Klack said mildly. He fixed a dark eye on her. "Things are not always what they seem."

That sounded very significant, Bentley thought, blinking back at the raven. Portentous. *Things are not always what they seem.* She'd have to think about it later. But right now, the most important thing on her mind was Cal.

"What are we going to do now?" Bentley asked.

"We?" Klack fluffed out his feathers, then let them slowly settle into place. "What do you mean *we*?"

"But I thought you were going to help!"

"I've done my bit. You have your memory and a clear head. Meddling is one thing. Doing your job for you is something else."

"My job?"

"Finding your courage." The raven lifted his wings and studied the feathers beneath them. "You don't give yourself enough credit."

"I keep failing!" Bentley said.

"Well," Klack gave his wings an experimental flap, "at least you keep trying. Now read your message, it's time for me to go."

"Message?" Bentley stared at the raven in confusion. Then she remembered the book in her hands. She'd been holding it open all this time without looking at the page marked inside. The message must be in the book!

Bentley looked down to see that the open white pages facing her were blank except for one neatly printed line.

Make it so.

Bentley frowned. She had expected more. Maybe some complex magic spell. Or some clue to how she might win against Mordicus. But this didn't tell her much of anything. Did it?

"Got it?" Klack asked. "Good."

And he was gone.

The book was gone too.

Bentley found herself simply standing alone in the middle of her room, hands poised to hold a book that wasn't there.

Knock, knock, knock. The rapping on her door made Bentley jump and her heart start pounding again. She rushed to open it, not knowing what to expect.

"Hi!" It was Uncle Rudy with his hair on end and a satisfied grin on his face. "Just thought I'd let you know I'm home."

Bentley threw herself at him and gave him a mighty hug around the middle from the pure relief of seeing him.

Uncle Rudy hugged her back. "Everybody should be greeted like this! It would probably lead to world peace. Have I done anything in particular to deserve it?"

"I'm just glad you're here." Bentley stepped back, still grinning. She was especially glad to be herself again with all her memory intact.

"I've got news!" Uncle Rudy tugged impatiently at the tie around his neck. "But I have to get out of these clothes first!"

"News about what?" Bentley followed her uncle down the hall to his room and watched as he rummaged through his big canvas duffel bag.

"Gardner." He was shuffling through sweatshirts and T-shirts and shorts when he suddenly pulled a framed photograph out of the bag. "Ha!" He looked at the photo, shook his head, and handed it over to Bentley.

In the silver frame was a posed picture of Uncle Rudy, Dr. Gardner, and another man. The three men were standing together on some kind of stage, all holding one large plaque and smiling at the camera. Dr. Gardner was in the middle, looking wise, gentle, and very dignified, Bentley thought. Uncle Rudy had a goofy grin and one arm hooked around Dr. Gardner's shoulders. The other man was smiling, but he looked stiff and uncomfortable. He was small and thin and stood a little apart, as if he were ready to run off at any moment. Shifty, Bentley decided.

"That was taken two years ago. The three of us were accepting an award on behalf of the department."

"Who's he?" Bentley pointed at the thin man.

Uncle Rudy made a scornful face. "Craven."

"Oh!" Bentley looked at him more closely. Definitely shifty. Dr. Craven had a pointy kind of face with small, nervous eyes. Mousy, Bentley thought. His hair, face, and clothes were a pale mouse color too.

Uncle Rudy hopped to his feet holding a bright red T-shirt and khaki shorts. "Be right back!" He ducked down the hall to the bathroom.

Bentley was curious about Dr. Craven and glad for a chance to study his picture. Here was somebody mean enough to want to ruin Dr. Gardner just to make himself more important. To have power. And that reminded her of Mordicus.

At the back of her mind, Bentley had been wondering if Mordicus might have something to do with Dr. Gardner's problem with words. Regular as clockwork, that's what Dr. Gardner had said about being ferhoodled. And that certainly reminded her of the clockwork Murdoch house that Mordicus had made. But even more, what made her think of Mordicus was the sly kind of humor in Dr. Gardner's problem. It had a mocking edge, Bentley thought, like the silent laughter Mordicus seemed to have for her. Too much power, Klack had said. Mordicus had been spoiled. And power seemed to be Dr. Craven's problem too.

"Flash!" Uncle Rudy sprang through the doorway. "A news bulletin!"

But just then Kate Bentley's voice came drifting up from the front hall. "Hello-o! I'm home!" The front door closed with a solid thunk.

"Up here!" Uncle Rudy yelled. He winked at Bentley. "Now I can get two birds with one stone."

A few moments later, Bentley's mom appeared in Uncle Rudy's bedroom doorway. She was still wearing her tennis ball costume, and the chartreuse ball made a wild contrast with her red cheeks. Her hair was almost as messy as Uncle Rudy's. "What's up?"

"Uncle Rudy was just about to deliver a news bulletin," Bentley explained as she carefully laid the framed photograph facedown on the bedroom carpet. As if that way, Craven wouldn't hear Uncle Rudy's news.

Bentley and her mom looked expectantly at Uncle Rudy.

"Tomorrow's the day," Uncle Rudy said. "The Showdown. Tomorrow the dean of the university will be arbitrating at Gardner's special meeting. It's going to be a long night, but by the end of it things should be settled once and for all."

"Whew!" Bentley's mom said. "Dr. Gardner certainly makes up his mind fast! Definitely Choice B."

Uncle Rudy looked confused, so Bentley tried to explain. "It's one of mom's Shakespeare quotes."

"Hamlet," Bentley's mom said.

"It's like this," Bentley said. "Hamlet's having a bunch of problems and worrying about—*whether 'tis nobler in the mind to, Choice A, suffer the slings and arrows of outrageous fortune or, Choice B, by opposing, end them.*"

Uncle Rudy started to laugh. "Gardner took Choice B! Of course!"

Me too, Bentley thought. I'm taking Choice B first thing tomorrow, just like Dr. Gardner. And I'm going to rescue Cal whether he wants me to or not.

13

That night Bentley could doze for only five or ten minutes at a time before she woke again with a start. She finally fell into a deep sleep just before dawn, and she slept late into the morning. It wasn't long after she got out of bed that Charles and Arthur rang the front doorbell.

"Arthur got worried," Charles explained as Bentley stepped out to the front porch. "So we figured we'd make sure you hadn't fainted again in front of a speeding car or collapsed in a coma someplace."

"I'm okay now," Bentley said.

"Oh?" Charles wiggled his eyebrows at her. "You mean you're not going to faint anymore when you hear Cal's name?"

Bentley made a face at him. "I won't even get dizzy."

"Good!" Arthur gave Bentley a sharp, encouraging

nod. "See you!" He jumped off the porch and loped toward Poplar Street, waving over his shoulder to them as he went.

"He's going into the city to see some photography exhibit," Charles said. "But first he wanted to make sure you weren't dead or anything."

"Well, I'm not." Bentley sank down on the top step of the porch.

Charles sat down beside her. "So? What was wrong with you?"

"It's going to sound weird," Bentley warned.

Charles nodded. "Then things are back to normal. By the way, I told Arthur about Cal being haunted and Mordicus and the Murdoch house."

"You told him?" Bentley started worrying. Sometimes Arthur took being older too seriously. "Will he tell your parents?"

Charles was indignant. "No way! I only told Arthur so he *wouldn't* talk to anybody else. He thought you had a brain tumor or something. I had to tell him it might be just magic."

Bentley snorted. *Just* magic. "Well, it was. I've been under a spell that Mordicus cast to make me forget about Cal and everything that happened. Everytime I tried to remember, my head started to pound and I couldn't think."

"You were under a spell?" Charles was delighted. "That's even better than fainting!"

She jumped up and began to pace. "But last night everything changed." Bentley told Charles about Klack and how she got her memory back and also about the message in the book. *Make it so.* "Now I've got to *do* something to get Cal away from Mordicus! Days have gone by and anything could have happened!"

Charles hummed a little, thinking. "It seems to me you've got two problems," he finally said. "One, what can a kid like you do against Mordicus and his magic?"

"There's got to be *something*!" Bentley refused to give up so easily. Klack seemed to think there was something she could do. If only she knew what it was!

Charles shrugged. "Okay, even if you can do something, there's problem number two. What if Cal doesn't want to be rescued?"

"He needs help whether he wants it or not!"

Charles was humming again.

Bentley glared at him. "Well? Are you going to help me?"

"Of course," Charles said mildly. "But this afternoon I have to take James Francis to the mall."

"Then we'll do it right now!" Bentley declared. "We'll go over to Cal's together and *make* him listen."

When they rang the doorbell at Cal's house a little while later, it was Cal's sister Leanne who answered. Cal wasn't home, she told them, and she didn't know when he'd be back. She didn't bother to say goodbye when she closed the door.

"It's hard to believe she was practically the most popular girl in the junior class," Charles said.

Worry was gnawing steadily at Bentley. Maybe it

was already too late to rescue Cal. "Let's try the electrical shop."

"I should be getting home for lunch," Charles said.

Bentley didn't spare him a look as she climbed onto her bike. She was going to the electrical shop. Period. Even if the thought of it made her stomach feel like a sick fish.

With a sigh, Charles caught up with her.

The sun was hot on Bentley's shoulders and the top of her head as they rode up Westfield to Poplar Street. When they turned the corner, Charles honked his *ca-yu-ga* horn and startled Bentley so that she nearly crashed her bike. Out of habit, she came to a stop at Canada's Drugstore. She felt better approaching the Mordicus Electrical Shop slowly.

Bentley led Charles across the street, past the bank, the Hallmark shop, and the Paris Beauty Salon. "It's the next store," she told him, staring straight ahead and readying herself to see Mordicus again as they passed Iario's Shoe Repair.

"Are you sure?" Charles asked. "I don't remember an electrical store down here."

Bentley stopped at the recessed doorway just before the alley. "This is it," she announced and turned to face the shop.

But there was no shop. She was facing a solid brick wall where the shop's window had been and a painted, padlocked wooden door instead of the glass door of Mordicus's shop. She looked up to see the sign. But the sign was gone.

"It was here!" Bentley turned to check her bearings. No doubt about it, this is where she and Cal had been. "There was a wooden sign with an eye and a lightning bolt! And a glass door with the name in gold paint! Mordicus Electrical Shop!"

Charles stepped back to study the front of the building, looking up and down the street with a frown of concentration. "This looks right to me, Bentley," he said. "I don't remember anything else being here."

"It was here!" Bentley insisted.

"Don't panic," Charles said. "It's probably on the next street or down a block or something."

"No!" Bentley insisted. "It was next to the shoe place!"

"Well, it couldn't be," Charles said reasonably, "because it's not here now."

How could the shop be gone? Bentley was staring at the blank wall when a man in a long, dark raincoat rushed out of the alley and collided with her. She took a swift, startled look at his face under a slouchy dark hat before he brushed past her and hurried down the street.

"Hey!" Bentley called after him. The man looked familiar. But why? He had a face like a weasel, she thought. Pointed and suspicious.

"Weird." Charles was staring after the heavily cloaked man too. "The sun is shining like crazy. Why is the guy wearing a hat and a raincoat?"

Bentley shrugged and shook herself. She had more important things to worry about. Like the electrical shop. What happened to it?

Magic, Bentley thought. That was the only explanation. "I'll bet the shop was only here so that Cal could find it and meet Mordicus. And now that Mordicus has got him, the shop is gone."

Charles gave a whistle of disbelief. "It's a lot more likely that you got the address wrong. You could just go home and look it up in the phone book."

"Geez, Charles, you and your phone book!"

Charles shrugged. "Do you have a better idea?"

Hard as she tried to think, Bentley didn't. She finally had to shake her head and admit it.

"Okay, then," Charles said. "There's nothing more we can do right now. But I've got to go home, and that's what I'm doing."

Charles was right, Bentley thought. There was nothing they could do, but she still felt lost.

"Why don't you come home with me?" Charles suggested. "We can have lunch at my house and then take James Francis to the mall."

Her only other choice, Bentley thought, was peanut butter and jelly alone at home. "Okay," she said. "Lunch and the mall. Then you can help me look for Cal again."

"It's a deal," Charles agreed.

Bentley was having tomato soup and grilled cheese sandwiches at the Donovans' big kitchen table when Mrs. Donovan came in from the garden with the first harvest of cucumbers and strawberries. She also had instructions for Charles about his trip to the mall with James Francis to pick up a new outfit for the two-year-old. "Be sure he tries it on and has plenty of wiggle room," Mrs. Donovan said.

They caught the bus to Burlington Mall on the corner of Colter Street with James Francis doing his best chimpanzee impression. He was still acting like a chimpanzee at Kids 'N Stuff, and Bentley wouldn't have believed how hard it was to buy clothes for one little kid.

When they were finally finished, standing outside the store and wondering what to do next, James Francis pointed dramatically to the far end of the mall.

"COOKIE!" he yelled.

Charles and Bentley turned to look. Small clusters of people were milling around folding tables and display booths at a Craft and Bake Sale. It was exactly the kind of situation where James Francis was bound to get into trouble. But James Francis had always had a kind of sixth sense about cookies and where to find them.

"COOKIE!" James Francis yelled again. His round face was beaming with joy.

Charles tried to tell him they'd get cookies later at home. But James Francis wouldn't listen.

"COOKIE! COOKIE! COOKIE!"

"Okay, okay, you win! Cookies!" Charles looked at Bentley and shrugged helplessly.

Bentley shrugged back. With Charles holding his brother's hand and James Francis impatiently tugging him forward, the three of them walked toward the sale. But as they got closer Bentley's stomach gave a warning flutter. She had a prickly, expectant feeling as if she were walking into a thunderstorm. Bentley slowed down, then stopped.

Charles turned to see what was keeping her.

"There's something *wrong* over there," Bentley said.

"Yeah, a bunch of wooden geese wearing bows and little brooms with dried-up flowers stuck on them."

"I mean really, Charles. I'm getting that same feeling I got about the Murdoch house."

Charles rolled his eyes. "A magic back sale."

"Cookies!" James Francis insisted.

"Okay, how about this," Charles said. "I'll just take James Francis over there, buy him a couple of cookies, and come right back. You can stay here and wait."

Bentley wanted to grab his arm and get him out of there fast. But Charles would just think she was nuts. And maybe she was. What could happen here with all these people around? "Okay," she agreed reluctantly. "But hurry up!"

"No problem." Charles let his little brother pull him into the crowd, and Bentley watched them slip into the shifting mass of people like stones disappearing under the surface of a river.

She waited. And kept waiting. How long could it take to buy a cookie? She twitched and shifted from foot to foot, getting more and more worried the longer she waited. Then, from the jittery feeling of electricity in the air and the nervous flutter in her insides, Bentley was suddenly sure that Charles and

James Francis must be in some kind of trouble, trouble that had to do with Mordicus.

She couldn't stand waiting any longer. Bentley marched into the small crowd of shoppers at the end of the mall, looking for the bakery table. But when she found it, there was no sign of Charles or James Francis.

Don't panic, she told herself, just look around. They must be here someplace. But where?

Bentley wound from table to table, squeezing between people up and down the aisles. No Charles. No James Francis.

Maybe by now they'd gone to where she was supposed to be waiting. Bentley ran to look, but they weren't there.

Her heart was thumping double-time as she crossed the mall again, back to the Craft and Bake Sale. She stood on the edge of the thinning crowd, trying to think of what to do next.

Here, something in her mind seemed to say, *look here.* Bentley took a deep breath to calm herself. She slowly scanned the booths and tables with their ruffled pillows, ceramic animals, dolls, and bake sale pies, cakes, and cookies. Then, on the far edge of the sale, she saw what she was looking for.

It was an empty booth with an empty brown folding table in front of a brown pegboard screen. There was something hanging on the pegboard, and Bentley walked slowly toward it. High in one corner of the pegboard hung a clock. It was a perfect miniature of the Mordicus Electrical Shop. Just like the shop, the clock was brown and square with a dusty window for its face and a tiny sign showing an eye in a triangle struck by lightning bolts.

As Bentley stared, the clock began to chime softly. On the stroke of three a light went on in the back of the shop. Seven . . . eight. A shadow passed in front of it, as if a tiny figure were walking by. Twelve . . . thirteen. The light went off. Bentley waited, hardly breathing. Now what?

But nothing else happened.

Bentley's mind began to race. So Mordicus *had* been here! What did that mean for Charles and James Francis? Had Mordicus kidnapped them? The idea made her stomach lurch and her throat close up. What would Mordicus want with them?

Bentley ran to the nearest neighboring booth. She asked a lady selling embroidered placemats if she had seen Charles and James Francis or Mordicus. But the lady said she'd been too busy to notice.

Maybe the clock would tell her something, Bentley thought.

She hurried back to the empty booth, but when she got there, the clock was gone. It had vanished, just like the electrical shop itself. Just like Charles and James Francis.

14

For a long time, Bentley refused to admit that the boys were gone. She searched almost every inch of the mall, just in case she had somehow missed them. By the time Bentley finally gave up, the mall was almost empty.

But Bentley had one last hope. Maybe Charles and James Francis were under the same spell of forgetfulness she had been under. Maybe Mordicus had simply sent them home and they were there right now eating dinner. With her fingers crossed, Bentley decided to call the Donovans' house from a pay phone and find out.

Arthur answered.

"Is Charles there?" Bentley tried not to sound particularly concerned.

"No. I thought he was supposed to be with you," Arthur said.

"Oh." Bentley's voice quavered. She couldn't help it. "I think it's Mordicus."

There was a long silence on the other end of the phone. Then Arthur said, "You better come over and tell me about it."

Bentley caught the bus from the mall to the Donovans' house where, Arthur had told her, he was home alone. When she arrived, Arthur was on the porch waiting for her. She sat with him on the porch steps, still warm from the sun, and began her story from the beginning, even though Charles had already told Arthur part of it. She told Arthur everything that happened through that afternoon at the mall, and he listened to every word without interrupting or asking questions.

"Well, that's it," Bentley said. "That's all I know." She waited for Arthur's reaction.

Arthur frowned, looking like Charles working on a difficult math problem. "Well, *something* must have happened to them. But magic at the mall is hard to believe."

Bentley gritted her teeth. Why did all of the Donovans have to be so practical? But, like her mom always said, believing is seeing. What she needed, Bentley decided, was some tangible proof to convince Arthur that magic really was at work.

"Cal has the clock," she said. "That's some kind of evidence. And he should be able to give us some answers, if we could find him!"

Arthur stood up. "What's his phone number?"

They called from the Donovans' kitchen. The

phone must have rung ten times at Cal's house before they finally got an answer.

Bentley grabbed the receiver. "Cal? It's me!"

"Hey." Cal's voice was thin and weak.

"What's wrong with you?" Bentley demanded. "What's going on?"

"I can't explain right now, but I need a car. Can you get one here?"

"A car? How am I supposed to get a car?"

"I can drive a car," Arthur said. "Sort of."

Bentley looked at him. "Sort of?"

"Hurry." Cal hung up.

She slowly replaced the telephone receiver. "Can you really drive?"

"I won't have my license for another four months." Arthur was turning pink. "But I've been practicing with the Merc in the driveway, and I've been out a few times with my dad."

"But could you drive by yourself? Won't you get in trouble?"

Arthur took a deep breath. "Charles and James Francis are my responsibility. If my driving the Merc is going to help find Mordicus and find them, then that's what I have to do." He got the keys to the Mercury, and they walked outside without another word.

Bentley's heart lifted a little when she saw the big green car in the driveway. Already the Mercury seemed like an old friend as she rested her hand on the sun-warmed metal.

"Let's go," Arthur said, and he climbed inside. The engine started with a gentle roar.

"All for one and one for all," Bentley said. She stepped in and pulled the door shut behind her.

Arthur stalled the car only once. He drove slowly, staying on side streets to avoid traffic and moving as steadily as a turtle toward Cal's house.

The windows in the old Mercury were small and set high, and the interior smelled of leather and polish. Bentley had to prop herself up in the plump seat just to see out. Even Arthur had to sit tall to see as he steered with both hands tightly gripping the wheel.

"You're doing great," Bentley told him.

Twilight was settling fast, and many houses already had their lights on. But Cal's house was completely dark when they pulled up to the curb, and it seemed deserted as Bentley and Arthur walked to Cal's front door. Bentley rang the doorbell and then knocked, but there was no answer. After a few moments, Arthur reached around her to knock more loudly. First he used his knuckles and then his fist to pound the heavy door. As he did, the door slowly swung open to an empty hallway.

"I guess it wasn't closed all the way," Bentley said. Where was Cal? She took a deep breath. "H-E-L-L-O!"

There was a thump and a muffled yelling from the direction of Isolation. Bentley and Arthur looked at each other. "From Cal's room, I think," Bentley said.

"Show me."

She led the way through the dark house to the hallway outside Cal's bedroom. The door to the room was closed, and she called his name.

"In here! Come in!"

Arthur cautiously eased the door open.

"Over here." Cal was hard to find at first in the dim bedroom. But his white-blond hair had its own soft radiance in the darkness. He was sitting on the floor, propped casually against the bed.

"Why didn't you answer the door?" Arthur said. "And what's the big emergency?"

"Hi, Arthur." Cal looked surprised to see him.

"Arthur drove," Bentley explained. "And he knows everything. Or everything that *I* know."

"I didn't know you could drive," Cal said. "Neat."

"Cal—" Bentley began impatiently.

But Cal held up one hand to stop her. "I know, you want to know what's going on. I needed the car," he said matter-of-factly, "because my legs quit working."

Bentley gawked at him. He was simply sitting there, looking calm and comfortable and maybe a little sheepish.

"Where's a phone?" Arthur asked. "I'll call Emergency."

"That won't help," Cal said.

"Ouch!" Bentley had come into the bedroom to kneel beside him and something sharp pressed into her bare knee. Now she noticed that the floor all around Cal was covered with sharp shards and fragments like shrapnel.

"What is this stuff? What's wrong with your legs? Why can't we call an ambulance?" Bentley asked.

"Just wait a minute, will you?" Cal seemed calm and in control. "Arthur, get that light switch over by the door."

Arthur found the switch and flipped it on. They all blinked at one another in the sudden bright light.

Bentley frowned down at the litter on the floor, and one of the pieces caught her eye. "It's the clock!" She snatched up a piece of the tiny broken turret from the model of the Murdoch house.

"Don't touch it!" The urgent note of warning in Cal's voice made her drop it as if it burned her fingers.

She looked at the pieces of clock with a half-formed suspicion. "Does the broken clock have something to do with your legs not working?"

Cal nodded. "I think so."

"Could you just explain this simply so I can understand it?" Arthur asked.

Cal sighed. "I guess being haunted and getting the clock and the book and meeting Mordicus was like getting swept up in a whirlwind. I couldn't seem to help it. And I was so proud when Mordicus chose *me* to be his apprentice."

"That's like getting happy about being chosen by Bluebeard," Bentley said.

"He's not *that* bad," Cal said. "But I finally figured out you were right, Bentley. It would be too easy to become just like him, misusing the power."

Bentley suddenly realized what Cal was saying. He didn't want to be Mordicus's apprentice! "You won't do it! Like you wouldn't fight Todd Lunden!"

Shadows flickered in Cal's gray-green eyes. "I learned that you don't really use power. You let the power use *you* while you try to channel it. But you need to be pure and strong. Mordicus isn't. He got bent somehow."

"Klack said all that power went to his head," Bentley said. Then she told Cal about the raven's visit and how she got back her memory and the headache disappeared. She kept the message in the red book and a lot of what Klack had said to herself. It was personal, she decided.

"Mordicus! I should have known!" Cal shook his head. "He told me you'd forget anything to do with him. He didn't say how he'd do it, but I should have asked! I'm really sorry, Bentley."

Bentley looked at the floor and shrugged, instantly forgiving him. He hadn't known!

"It took me too long to figure out, but when I finally realized how Mordicus was and how he saw people as things to use, I left him."

"And he let you?" Arthur looked doubtful.

"Not exactly," Cal said ruefully. "This morning, when I told Mordicus I didn't want to be his apprentice anymore, he didn't look too surprised. I guess I'd started asking a lot of questions and telling him what I thought. So he just smiled and said something about not counting all my rabbits before they came out of the wrong hat. And he said changing hats wasn't so easy. Then he said it didn't matter, because I'd be back."

"Cryptic," Bentley said. "And smug."

"The first thing I did when I got home," Cal went on, "was to smash the clock. I figured he'd know and get the message. I even stomped all over it."

"And then something happened to your legs?" Arthur guessed.

"Not right away. But after a while it felt as if my toes were asleep. Then my feet were kind of numb. Then the numbness started creeping up my legs. Now I can't feel them at all or get them to move."

"But what about my brothers?" Arthur asked.

Cal looked confused. "What about them?"

"We think Mordicus has Charles and James Francis." Bentley told Cal about how the boys disappeared at the mall and how she had seen the chiming clock shaped like the Mordicus Electrical Shop.

"A mysterious disappearance and a disappearing clue. That sounds like Mordicus, all right." Cal looked thoughtful.

"But why would he do it?" Arthur asked.

"Hostages, I'll bet," Bentley said.

"I think you're right," Cal said. "Maybe he wants to do a trade. Me for them."

"But where is he hiding them?" Bentley asked. "The shop is gone!"

"Elementary, my dear Bentley." Cal grinned. "At the Murdoch house."

"Oh!" Of course, Bentley thought. That was where everything had started! "Does Mordicus live there? Was he really Murdoch all along?"

"Mordicus takes many different identities." Cal sounded like Uncle Rudy. "He travels a lot."

"But the house is for sale! It's supposed to be empty!"

"It's only a passageway, a door to elsewhere." Cal had begun to look impatient. "We should get going now. I don't know how much time I have left."

"What do you mean?" Bentley jumped up to help Arthur as he hoisted Cal to his feet.

"The numbness in my legs is still spreading."

"Oh, no!" Bentley was horrified. But Cal seemed calm and almost cheerful.

"I'm not going to let Mordicus push me around," Cal said as they hauled him to his feet. "No matter what he does to me, he can't win."

Bentley and Arthur made a fireman's chair for Cal, linking their crossed hands to make a seat.

"But what will happen to Charles and James Francis?" Arthur asked.

Cal frowned. "I don't know."

"If we just stand here, nothing is going to happen!" Bentley snapped. Her arms were already starting to ache with Cal's weight.

"Let's go," Arthur said, and they carried Cal through the dark house, winding carefully around the designer furniture, across the plush carpeting, and all the way out.

Cal's eyes lit when he saw the Mercury. "What is it?"

"A 1949 Mercury," Bentley informed him. "A classic."

Bentley and Arthur moved Cal into the front seat, giving him the middle spot between them. "You'd better drive to my house first," Bentley told Arthur as he guided the car onto the empty street. "I'll get my mom's keys."

Ten minutes later, Bentley was thinking how easy it was to slip her mom's keys out and away. It was odd to think how scared she had been about doing the same thing just a few days ago. Of course, that was different. It was before Charles and James Francis were kidnapped and Cal's legs were turned numb and useless.

On her way out, Bentley paused at the foot of the stairs, thinking of Uncle Rudy's clay pot of red ocher and the quiet earth magic it held. It was the perfect thing to take with them to face Mordicus.

Maybe somehow it would protect them, Bentley thought as she climbed the stairs. It could remind her of Uncle Rudy and being brave and solving your own problems. And maybe, she thought as she closed her hand around the small, rough clay pot, maybe it would just be something handy to throw the next time she saw Mordicus.

15

Bentley was in and out of her house and back to the Mercury in just over three minutes with the keys to the Murdoch place in one hand and her clay pot in the other.

"Tell me more about the Murdoch house," Arthur said to Cal as he shifted the car into gear. "Why'd you call it a passageway?"

"Mordicus says it's a place where the walls are thin."

"Walls?" He didn't mean the walls of the house, Bentley figured.

"Mordicus told me magic used to be a natural part of the world," Cal said. "But humans pushed magic out. Mordicus says we did it because people like things neat and orderly. And small enough to control. But true magic isn't small and neat. True magic is a wild power, and it made people nervous."

"How did they get rid of it?" Arthur asked.

"By refusing to believe in it," Cal said. "And by making up rules like the law of gravity. It got so there wasn't any room for the wild power, and it went back into the Great Chaos where it came from in the first place. But even now, there's still some wild magic left between the cracks."

"*Between the Cracks*! That's the name of that book!"

Cal nodded. "Dakin's book. It was his journal and a record of everything he knew about magic and how to use it. Dakin was Mordicus's old master, and he was very powerful. But he disappeared years ago, and Mordicus never found out what happened to him."

"Between *what* cracks exactly?" Arthur asked.

Cal frowned. "Mordicus talked for hours about the origins of power and the divided worlds. Then he said that was only the beginning of basic theory. It's not much, but I'll tell you what I know. The Great Chaos surrounds the human world. It's a whole other reality that's a lot different from ours. And in between our world and the Great Chaos, there's another world, a sort of buffer zone where magic still exists."

"Between the cracks!" Bentley said.

"Right. Mordicus can slip between the cracks anytime he wants. But it's especially easy to do where the walls between the worlds are thin. Like in the Murdoch house."

"Have you been there?" Arthur asked.

"Yes," Cal said.

He wants to go back, Bentley thought. He misses the magic already.

"What if Mordicus took Charles and James Francis there?" Arthur was easing the Mercury around the corner of Riverview Drive. "Could we go in after them?"

"I can get us between the cracks," Cal said, "but that's just the beginning. It's a kind of half-world there, without any shape of its own. If you can use the power, you can shape it the way you want. I was just beginning to learn how."

Arthur made a worried noise.

"Look, Arthur, I don't think Mordicus is going to hurt them," Cal said. "He's not really evil. He's just forgotten how to be human."

Bentley snorted in disbelief. There was Cal with legs that wouldn't work and a creeping numbness taking over his whole body, talking about how Mordicus wasn't really that bad!

"We're here," Arthur announced as he guided the Mercury to the curb. He turned off the engine and headlights as Bentley and Cal turned to look at the Murdoch house.

The house was only a darker shadow among the trees. Bleak and empty, Bentley thought. In fact, all of Riverview Drive seemed deserted, with no people in sight, no cars passing in the soft summer night. And the only thing she could hear was the sound of crickets and cicadas.

"I'm going in alone first to check the place out," Arthur announced. "I need the key, Bentley."

Bentley bounced to attention and turned to glare at him. Maybe she was a chicken sometimes and maybe she messed things up, but she wasn't just going to sit out here while Arthur took charge and did everything! "I'm going with you!"

"No, you're not."

"You can't stop me!"

Arthur opened his mouth, then shut it. He shook his head. "You're right. I can't."

"Me too," Cal said. "You need me."

Arthur chewed his bottom lip, thinking hard. "For a scouting party, this whole thing is getting out of hand. I can't stop Bentley from coming," he told Cal, "but if she and I have to carry you in, we won't be able to go in quietly or get out fast. It's better if you stay here for now."

Cal shook his head in exasperation. "You don't understand! You can't sneak up on Mordicus or surprise him. He's got listeners in the wind. He can see a thousand miles, and he already knows we're here. When you go in, you'll just be walking into something he's got set up and waiting for you!"

"A trap?"

"He could do anything," Cal said. "And I mean *anything*. Mordicus likes to play tricks and games. You've got to take me with you!"

But Arthur shook his head. "If Mordicus is that powerful, then taking you in there would be the same as handing you over. I won't do that." He opened the Mercury door. "We'll be back."

"Wait!" Bentley cried. "There's something I have to do first!"

It was the clay pot, warm and solid in her hands,

that gave her the idea and Uncle Rudy's stories about how the people of the outback would call on the Dreamtime spirits and summon their earth magic. Bentley carefully pried the wax lid off her clay pot. She dipped her fingers into the soft red dust, feeling both solemn and silly, then drew a line of ocher across Arthur's forehead and slashes on his cheeks.

"For protection," Bentley said.

Arthur grinned. "War paint!" He reached two fingers into the dust, then traced a wavy line across Bentley's forehead.

"How do we look?" Arthur asked Cal.

"Pretty amazing," Cal said glumly.

"Here." Bentley held out the clay pot. "Put some on."

Cal shook his head and shrugged. "Why not?" He tapped a finger in the red ocher, then slashed lines across his forehead and cheeks.

"Let's go." Arthur climbed out of the car and closed the door firmly behind him.

Bentley's heart was pounding as she reached for the door handle.

"Bentley!" Cal's voice made her pause halfway out of the car. "Remember, you have more power than you know."

"Me?"

Cal nodded as he closed his eyes and sank back into the soft leather seat. "You."

He was probably just trying to make her feel better, Bentley thought as she backed out of the car. She closed the car door with a solid clunk.

The Mercury deserved protection too, Bentley thought, and she reached back inside the open window to retrieve the clay pot as Arthur came around to stand beside her.

"We need a flashlight." He leaned through her open window to rummage in the glove compartment, and while Arthur searched, Bentley sprinkled red dust all over the Mercury's hood, top, sides, trunk, and even the tires.

She made a complete circle all the way around the car. "There!" Bentley nodded to herself with satisfaction as she returned the clay pot to the front seat.

Arthur had found a flashlight and stood waiting patiently for her. "Stay here," he said. "I'm going in alone. Just give me the key."

"No." Bentley turned and marched to the iron gate that guarded the Murdoch house with Arthur right behind her.

He reached for the latch, but as he touched the metal he gave a startled cry and pulled his hand away quickly.

"It's ice cold!" Arthur looked at his hand in wonder. "My fingers stuck to it!"

"Mordicus." He likes to play tricks, Bentley remembered.

Arthur hummed thoughtfully and used the flashlight to lift the latch and push the gate open.

Bentley kept waiting for something to happen as they walked up the sidewalk to the house. She half expected a great flash of lightning to strike them when she put the key in the lock of the front door.

But the door swung open easily, and everything was still as they stepped inside.

Arthur used the flashlight to cast a puny circle of light around the empty living room.

"Upstairs," Bentley whispered. "If they're here, I'll bet they're in the turret room."

Arthur glanced at her, then did a double take. "Your face!"

Bentley turned to look at him. In the reflected glow of the flashlight, she could see a sparkling streak like stars dashed across his forehead and cheeks.

"The dust!" It was shining with a light of its own in the darkness.

Arthur gave a little whistle. "Let's keep going."

Maybe it will make us look formidable, Bentley thought as she led the way ahead. She hoped so, anyway.

Arthur took the lead on the twisted stairway, shining the circle of light before them. Halfway up the stairs, Bentley caught a faint scent and almost missed her footing. It was the sharp and spicy smell of the electrical shop, growing stronger as they climbed.

They followed the spicy scent to the top of the stairs, then stopped while Arthur flashed the light around the hall. The dim beam caught something. At first it looked like a pile of old clothes heaped against the wall. But it was a man, Bentley saw, a man wearing a dark raincoat and a floppy hat. He was propped at an awkward angle against the wall near the door to the turret room.

"Do you think he's dead?" Bentley whispered.

Arthur moved to the dark figure and bent close. His flashlight lit the man's face. "He's breathing," Arthur said. "But I think he's unconscious."

Bentley blew out the breath she'd been holding and moved to Arthur's side, keeping her eyes on the slouching man.

"Is it Mordicus?" Arthur asked.

Bentley stared at the pale, pointed face beneath the dark hat. "No. But I think I know him." She recognized him as the man who'd been in the alley after the electrical shop disappeared. But even back then he looked familiar, Bentley thought. Where else had she seen him? Then she knew! He was in the photograph in Uncle Rudy's room. "It's Dr. Craven!"

"Who?"

Arthur already knew part of the story from Charles, and Bentley quickly explained the rest. "But what's he doing here?" she wondered out loud. What could Dr. Craven have to do with Mordicus?

Arthur looked grim. "Maybe he's been kidnapped too."

Bentley scowled at Craven. "Maybe." She thought of how Dr. Craven was trying to ruin Dr. Gardner. And how Dr. Gardner's mysterious problem with words always happened on the hour and half hour. Just like clockwork. Maybe a clock that Mordicus had made!

"Listen!" Arthur hissed. "Do you hear something?"

She could hear it. There was a sound . . . coming from inside the turret room. Bentley and Arthur traded a look, then both leaned closer to the door.

Arthur grinned at her. "It's James Francis! I recognize his snoring!"

Arthur cautiously eased the door open, and the strong scent of spice and electricity flowed over them like a cloud. Bright moonlight filled the turret room and showed them the curving walls and the huge curio cabinet. And there on the floor, a few feet in front of the curio, were Charles and James Francis curled up together like two puppies taking a nap.

It was too easy, Bentley thought. A warning prickled up her spine. They're like cheese in a mousetrap. And we're the mice.

Arthur rushed into the room to kneel beside his brothers while Bentley waited for the trap to spring.

Nothing happened.

She let herself relax a little. Maybe they were lucky. Maybe Mordicus had slipped off between the cracks for a few minutes and they'd be in and out before he knew it.

Bentley tiptoed into the turret room as Arthur gently shook Charles and whispered his name. Arthur shook harder. And even harder. But Charles and James Francis stayed as soundly asleep as Dr. Craven. It wasn't going to be so easy after all.

"Wake up!" Arthur said loudly as he rolled Charles over onto his back. Still no response. Arthur frowned at Bentley. "Do you think they're drugged or something?"

"Probably *or something*," Bentley said.

"Let's get them out of here," Arthur said. "You can carry James Francis, and I'll take Charles."

Bentley hesitated. This was as useless as rescuing a couple of sacks of potatoes. What good would it do if they couldn't wake the boys up?

Arthur was already on his feet with Charles draped across one shoulder. "What are you waiting for?"

"I think this is exactly what Mordicus wants us to do!"

Arthur scowled. "I'm not leaving without my brothers. We *could* just sit here and wait, but that would leave Cal alone and unprotected. And we'd be forced to meet Mordicus on his home ground. Or we can take these two with us and have a showdown where *we* choose!"

He had a point, Bentley thought. If they took Charles and James Francis with them, at least they'd all be together. Even if two of them were sound asleep and snoring and another one was going numb from the feet up.

"Okay," she said. "Let's get out of here."

They stopped at Dr. Craven's limp form in the hallway. "What do you think?" Arthur asked. "Should we try to come back for him?"

Bentley chewed her bottom lip in thought. His being here was a puzzle, but her intuition was telling her that Dr. Craven was nothing but trouble. Silently she shook her head.

Arthur sighed. "Okay, we'll leave him. But let's at least put him in a more comfortable position."

They got Dr. Craven stretched out on his back, then carried the sleeping boys down the dark stairway and out of the house. As they closed the door of the

Murdoch house behind them, they could hear Dr. Craven snoring loudly.

A few moments later, Arthur had the rear door of the Mercury open and was lowering Charles's limp body to the seat. Bentley's arms were beginning to ache with the warm weight of James Francis, and Cal was impatiently pouring out questions from the front seat.

"What happened? Are they okay? Did you see Mordicus?"

"Wait until we're on our way out of here." Arthur took James Francis from Bentley to deposit him on the seat with Charles. "Then we'll tell you everything."

They got the sleeping boys quickly arranged, and as the Mercury pulled onto the deserted street, Bentley told Cal everything that had happened.

"Craven?" Cal shook his head. "I never heard anything about him. It's just as well you left him there. But I don't know what we're going to do about Charles and James Francis."

"We figured we'd wait and see if we hear from Mordicus," Bentley said.

"Oh," Cal said softly. "We will. You can bet we will."

16

Bentley didn't even want to think about what awful things Mordicus might do. Fortunately, Cal didn't say another word as they drove down Riverview. In the silence, Bentley looked out at the houses passing by. But there was something odd going on out there, Bentley thought. "Look!" she said. "Look at that!"

Cal scanned the passing view. "Look at what?"

"Everything!" Bentley scowled out the window. "There's something wrong with the street."

She had been down this road a thousand times before, but it never looked like this. Everything was out of kilter. The street was too wide and too empty. The poles of the street lamps were too thin and spindly and much taller than they should be. And the lights themselves shone a dim, sickly yellow. As they drove past, the houses retreated more and more into the distance until they were only small, dark shapes at the back of far-stretching lawns.

"Look at the car!" Cal pointed at the broad hood of the Mercury.

The hood outside the front window was shimmering and sparkling like a field of stars. It was the red ocher dust, Bentley thought. She turned to look at Cal and Arthur. The dust on their faces was sparkling too.

"You said the dust was shining inside the Murdoch house," Cal said thoughtfully. "It probably shines whenever there's power around, and you can be pretty sure there's power here now. That means Mordicus is at work, sending us exactly where he wants us."

We didn't get away at all, Bentley thought. She watched the view out the window twist and change as if they were driving into a fun-house mirror. "Is this it?" she asked. "Are we between the cracks?"

"We never went there by car before," Cal said, "but it's sure starting to look like it."

"What do you think I should do?" Arthur sounded calm, but worried. The Mercury was moving at a crawl.

All around them, the streetlamps, trees, and houses of what used to be Riverview Drive were now just squiggles and blobs, blending into the darkness and disappearing. All around them the dense air and shadowy forms were the deep, dusky color of summer night. We might as well be driving in space, Bentley thought. And with a lurch of her stomach, she suddenly realized they were. They had arrived. They were between the cracks.

"Something's coming." Cal's voice held a soft warning. "Brace for it."

The world changed again.

The Mercury dropped a few feet through nothingness to land with a thunk on solid ground. The impact bounced Bentley hard in the soft leather seat. She grabbed the dashboard for balance with one hand while her other hand flailed toward Cal. Bright light flooded the car, and Bentley squeezed her eyes shut.

After a few moments, when everything was still and quiet, she cautiously opened her eyes again.

The world was orange. At least, everything outside the Mercury was. There was a sort of landscape out there, all rolling and lumpy like dough as far as Bentley could see in every direction. The doughy landscape was a kind of muddy carrot color, and the sky was a sort of murky pumpkin.

Cal sighed. "It's Mordicus. Orange is his favorite color."

Of course, Bentley thought. Leave it to Mordicus to take a perfectly good color like orange and turn it mucky.

"Something's coming." Arthur was looking into the rearview mirror. Now he leaned out the Mercury window for a better view while Bentley craned around in the seat to look out the back window.

What it looked like, Bentley thought, was a mechanical mouse, the size of a small tank, zigzagging toward them over the doughy hills.

"I can't see!" Cal couldn't budge his numb legs. He was still as stone from the waist down, Bentley thought, as though he were carved from marble.

"It's a mouse!" she told him. Arthur was already shifting gears on the Mercury and hitting the gas to get them out of there.

"A mouse?"

"Kind of silly looking. But it's made out of metal and it's big and fast." They had to get away, Bentley thought. Why weren't they moving?

"We're stuck." This time, Arthur sounded very worried.

Cal frowned, then nodded to himself. "There's no road," he said. "We haven't made one."

"Then let's do it!" Bentley said. The mouse was taking its time now, making leisurely loops and figure eights around the hills as it swooped and rattled toward the Mercury. It had an old-fashioned, ratchety kind of gait, as if cogs and gears were turning to make it move. Like the workings of an old clock, Bentley thought. "You can make a road, can't you, Cal?"

Cal sighed and settled back in his seat. "It takes a lot of energy. I'm not sure I've got it."

"We'll help," Bentley said.

"*Can* we help?" Arthur asked.

Bentley was keeping an eye on the tin mouse. It was playing with them now, moving closer and then away. Mordicus was probably having a lot of fun, Bentley thought, feeling smug and laughing at them. More than anything, she wished she could do something to let him know he wasn't as all-powerful as he thought. "Can't we do anything?"

Cal grimaced and shook his head. Then he stopped, thinking. "Maybe there *is* something. Mordicus said everyone has power. 'Power is as free as air,' he said, 'but most of those fools never feel its presence. Only a rare few have the talent or wit to use it.' "

Bentley made a face. "That sounds like Mordicus all right." Scornful. Arrogant and full of himself.

"The point is," Cal said, "everybody has power. Including you two. Maybe I can add your power to mine to get us out of here."

"I'll try anything," Arthur said. "What do we have to do?"

"Mostly, just relax," Cal said. "Settle back, close your eyes, and reach deep inside yourself for the power, as if you were reaching into your dreams. I'll be there too."

"Whatever you say." Arthur was already settling back in the soft seat. "We just better hurry."

Bentley closed her eyes and rested her head against the cool leather seat. There was power inside her, Cal had said, and Bentley tried to feel it there.

Cal's voice came soft and low. "There is a hidden place within you that's the source of all things, all energy, all power. Imagine finding that place, deep within you, and opening it, finding strength, finding everything you need."

Into Bentley's mind came the image of an old stone well. She let her thoughts travel down, through light and shadow and the cool green water, to the well's deepest depths. Where the power was. Her power. She could feel it now like an underground current, part of a river that ran through all creation. She could sense Arthur in the stream, slow and steady. She could even pick up a faint and faraway sense of Charles and James Francis. And she could feel Cal, cutting a path toward the light of the surface, up to where the power could be used to shape the formless world between the cracks.

Bentley slowly opened her eyes, feeling as if she were dreaming, afraid to wake herself up.

"Drive," Cal said.

Arthur stepped on the gas and the Mercury took off on the road their power had made.

17

Bentley started to wish she was in the back snoring with Charles and James Francis. Beside her, Cal was lying limp as seaweed against the seat. She wasn't even sure he was conscious.

"Does anybody have any suggestions?" Arthur asked. "Because I'd sure like to hear them." His knuckles were turning white as he gripped the steering wheel.

What were they going to do? Bentley's hand crept into the pocket of her shorts and closed around Uncle Rudy's clay pot for comfort. It seemed as if the rolling land was just waiting to be wakened, she thought. If only she knew how! What was it Cal said? Something about how reaching for magic was like reaching into dreams. Dreaming.

And then a thought came to her, clear and perfect.

"We should sing," Bentley announced.

"Sing?" Arthur shot a glance at the rearview mirror. The mouse was closing the distance. "You want to sing *now?*"

Bentley tried to explain her idea. "This place between the cracks is a lot like the Dreamtime Uncle Rudy talked about, the time when heroes made the Dreaming Trails. They made things by singing!"

Arthur frowned at the lumpy hills. Cal made a small bubbling sound and struggled to sit up.

"Oh, well," Arthur said, "why not?" He thought a moment, cleared his throat, and began to sing. *"There's no place like ho-ome,"* Arthur sang in a clear, mellow voice. *"There's no-o place like home. Be it ever so humble, there's no-o place like home."*

Leave it to a Donovan, Bentley thought, to come up with such a corny song. Holy cow. She took a deep breath and joined in. *"There's no place like ho-ome, there's no-o place like home,"* Bentley sang. She could feel Cal stir beside her.

"Be it ever so humble," Cal sang softly, *"there's no-o place like home."*

Arthur let the Mercury slow down. All their energy and attention went to their song and to thinking about home. They started the song again from the beginning, singing more strongly, and as they traveled, the land around them began to change.

The empty horizon filled with soft shapes. The landscape began to take on color. They went on singing while trees and flowers and garbage cans took form. They shaped green grass, a red brick house, a gas station, a corner store, and parking meters in a neighborhood Bentley almost recognized. And they kept on singing.

Soon the road was crowded with houses. And the houses, Bentley noticed, were all on one side of the street just as they were on Riverview Drive. Across the way were trees, underbrush, and the river. It looked almost normal, except for the half-twilight glow in the air and the fact that nothing was moving. Even the leaves on the dusty trees were perfectly still and waiting.

Finally they came to a curve that Bentley recognized with a certainty that settled in her stomach like a brick. Just around the curve, Bentley knew, was the Murdoch house. And that's what they'd been waiting for all along. She knew now that they had to go back to where it all started so they could finally finish it.

Bentley stopped singing. "Good!"

All this time she had been afraid of Mordicus. But she was sick and tired of feeling helpless and being pushed around. It was time to change things. *Make it so,* the message in the red book said. And like Uncle Rudy and Klack had both said, she was going to have to do it herself.

Cal fell silent, and Arthur's voice trailed off at the end of a line. With a sigh, he slowed the Mercury and pulled up to the curb across the street from the Murdoch house.

As they came to a stop, Bentley saw the tin-plated mouse roll up and park across the way. The air around the mouse began to shimmer, rippling like hot air over a blacktop highway. The shape of the mouse wavered and changed, stretching and darkening, forming a long hood and fins, becoming smooth and shiny until, in a matter of seconds, it had been transformed into a sleek black car with smoked windows.

"Wow. It's a 1962 Coupe de Ville Cadillac in mint condition." Arthur sounded awestruck.

"It's Mordicus!" she hissed at him.

"I know," Arthur said. "But it's still a great car."

Cal struggled feebly to push himself upright in the soft seat. "Tell Mordicus he can have me," Cal said. "Then he'll let you all go."

"No way!" Arthur said.

But Bentley regarded Cal thoughtfully. His strength was almost gone and soon he might be completely paralyzed. She would rather see him become Mordicus's apprentice, even if she lost him as a friend, than to have him stay like this or worse.

"Maybe Mordicus isn't so bad," Bentley said. "You'll learn a lot from him."

"I didn't say I'd cooperate with him!" Cal gathered enough energy to fire at her. "But I got you into this and I have to get you out!"

"Oh, for heaven's sakes! We've been through this before. We're all in it together, so stop trying to be noble and heroic!"

"Quite right." A harsh voice from Bentley's open window startled them. It was Klack, the raven, perched on the frame of the door, gripping it with strong blue-black claws, and cocking his sleek, dark head at them. He turned a bright black eye toward

Bentley and winked. "I've been sent to extend an invitation. Mordicus would like to have a rendezvous out in the street. If you ask me, he's seen too many cowboy movies."

"Cal can't walk," Bentley said.

Klack made a *tsk*-ing sound and shook his head. "Mordicus always goes too far. It's certainly no way to treat the power."

"Can you help us?" Arthur asked.

"Me? I'm just a talking raven."

Things are not always what they seem. Bentley remembered how significant that sounded when Klack said it to her. She was sure that there was more to Klack than they could see. But that wouldn't do them any good unless he chose to reveal himself. "Never mind," Bentley said. "This is something we've got to do ourselves."

"Ah!" Klack snapped his beak approvingly, nodded his dark head, and flew away in a rush of blue-black wings.

Bentley and Arthur looked at each other. Without a word, he opened his door and came around to her side of the Mercury. She climbed out, and the two of them moved Cal around so that his legs hung out the open door while he leaned sideways, supported by the seat. They stood on either side of him so that they could all face the black Coupe de Ville together.

Bentley's stomach was flopping like a fish, and her hands felt cold and clammy. But, she told herself, if she was ever going to be able to think of herself as a worthwhile person, she had to stand up to Mordicus now.

Seconds passed while Bentley forgot to breathe. Then the rear door of the Cadillac opened and Mordicus stepped out, smiling as if he had already won.

"A very entertaining chase," Mordicus said. "Now, shall we talk business?"

"What have you done to Charles and James Francis?" Arthur demanded.

Mordicus blinked at him with a surprised, innocent expression. "Didn't they snore before?"

"Wake them up, Mordicus," Cal said in a low, steady voice.

The Dark Man turned to look at Cal and lost his smug, superior expression. He looked sad, Bentley thought in surprise. He reminded her of a kid standing at the edge of a playground all alone, watching other kids play. *He's lonely,* Klack had said, and Bentley could see it now. But she still refused to feel sorry for him.

"Cal doesn't want to be your apprentice," Bentley said. "And you don't deserve to have him. You're mean and selfish and you don't care about anybody except yourself! And how low can you be to cast a spell on a two-year-old kid?"

"She's got you there!" Klack cawed from the hood of the Cadillac.

"Be quiet!" Mordicus snapped at the bird. "I've heard enough nonsense. Cal, say good-bye to your friends. We're going."

Arthur and Bentley both stepped forward to stand between Cal and Mordicus. "He's not going anywhere," Arthur said.

Bentley's hand closed on the clay pot in the roomy pocket of her shorts. She pulled it from her pocket. If only she could use the dust! Earth magic, Uncle Rudy had called it.

Bentley concentrated all her will on the red ocher and reached for the power inside herself. She remembered the message in the red book. *Make it so!* As Mordicus started toward them, she threw the pot as hard as she could.

The clay pot somersaulted through the air, arcing over the street, moving more and more slowly on its path to Mordicus. The wax seal flew out of the mouth of the pot and a cloud of red dust escaped. But instead of sifting to earth, the ocher dust swirled and hovered and thickened in midair.

The cloud of dust began to shape itself and settle to the ground. And when it touched the earth, the cloud had become a lion, as red as the desert, solid as flesh and stone. Smooth muscles moved across the lion's haunches and shoulders, and a deep warning rumble came from his throat as he blocked Mordicus's way.

Bentley watched the lion in wonder. She hadn't planned to make a lion. She hadn't been thinking anything in particular, just that she needed to protect them all.

Mordicus spoke a word in the liquid syllables of water moving over stone, and the air around him crackled with electricity. He was so sure his spell would work that his eyes were on Cal, not on the lion, when he started walking forward again. But his spell failed.

Bentley's lion sprang and caught Mordicus in the chest with his heavy paws. Bentley could hear The Dark Man's head strike concrete as he fell and heard his breath rush out. The lion crushed him to the ground and raised a heavy paw to strike.

"STOP!" Bentley screamed.

And the lion was gone.

18

Mordicus was still breathing. Bentley could see his chest rise and fall, so her lion hadn't killed him. But he wasn't moving.

Arthur whistled. "Killer dust!"

Bentley felt awful. She had only wanted to protect her friends, not really hurt him. What if Mordicus had a fractured skull? Or crushed ribs? Or a broken back?

She had to find out. "I'm going to see if he's okay."

"I'll go with you," Arthur said, and Bentley didn't argue.

As they started toward Mordicus's still form in the center of the road, Klack fluttered off his perch on the Coupe de Ville and flew to land beside The Dark Man. Bentley and Arthur stopped a few steps away to study Mordicus. His eyes were open, blinking up at the pumpkin-colored sky, and it seemed to Bentley that he looked thoughtful but not uncomfortable. He was covered with a fine sifting of red ocher dust.

"Mordicus?" Bentley said softly. "Are you all right?"

Mordicus blinked but didn't answer.

"Mordicus?" She moved closer. Arthur reached for her arm just as the air began to tingle against her skin and the spicy smell of electricity rushed over her.

There was a flash of darkness around the bearded man. And suddenly she was looking down at a box turtle about the size of a dinner plate, powdered in red dust, lying on its back in the road and craning its head to blink up at them.

The expression in the turtle's dark eyes was wild surprise. He flailed his stringy legs and long-necked beaky head for a few tense seconds, trying to get to his feet, then gave up and disappeared into his shell.

"Wow!" Arthur shook his head in admiration. "You're getting really good at this, Bentley!"

"But I didn't do it!" She stared at the upturned turtle, bewildered.

A modest cough sounded. "That was my work, actually."

Bentley and Arthur both jumped, startled by the new voice. It was Klack, Bentley realized. She frowned at the black bird. The voice had come from Klack, but it didn't sound like his clattering, scratchy raven's voice. This voice was deep and mellow.

As she watched, the air around the bird began to shimmer and blue sparks flickered over his sleek black body. The sparks flared so bright that Bentley had to squeeze her eyes shut. She smelled electricity.

"Hey," Arthur said quietly a moment later, and Bentley opened her eyes.

A tall stranger stood where Klack had been. The stranger had white hair, a long white beard, and bright black eyes. He was dressed in a blue-black robe that shimmered when he moved.

He was a stranger, Bentley thought, but she was sure she knew him. *"Things are not always what they seem!"* she quoted the raven. "It *is* you, isn't it?"

The stranger cocked his head and raised his eyebrows in a question.

"You're Klack." He *was* Klack, standing here now in human form. But there was more to him than that. She had a hunch about who he really was, and in some way felt as if she'd known it all along. "And you're Dakin."

The white-haired stranger nodded approval at her. "Trust your intuition, that's what I always say."

The box turtle peeped out of its shell to look at Dakin. His movement caught Dakin's eye, and he scowled down. "My prize pupil," Dakin said. "What a stinker."

Bentley followed his gaze to the turtle lying helplessly on its back. Mordicus *was* a stinker, but looking at him now, she was starting to feel sorry for him. And she wanted to cheer Dakin up about his choice of apprentices. "You and Cal both said he wasn't really so bad underneath it all," Bentley reminded him. "He just got carried away with having too much power and feeling all alone."

The turtle turned his cool stare to her, blinking slowly. He looked grateful, Bentley thought. Although it was hard to read emotion on a turtle's face.

"Things were always too easy for Mordicus," Dakin said. "It's time he learned a few lessons. Getting his comeuppance from you, Bentley, was a very good start." Dakin leaned down, talking in slow, clear tones to the turtle-Mordicus. "You see? First you're knocked off your high horse by a girl with no training at all, and when the lion she created could have pulverized you, she chose to spare you. Now she's taking pity on you. What do you say to that?"

Mordicus drew his head slowly back into his shell.

He was embarrassed, Bentley thought. Abashed. Good word. Or maybe he was just pouting.

"Can you help my brothers and Cal?" Arthur asked.

Dakin raised his hand to regard Arthur with one bright eye. "When the time is right, your brothers will wake up feeling fresh and clearheaded. As for Cal, I'd like to undo a lot of what Mordicus has done." He turned another scowling look down to his ex-student, still hiding in his shell. "You've made a terrible disgrace of yourself lately, Mordicus. And you misquote me constantly. You've corrupted everything I ever taught you."

Dakin drew himself up tall and directed his dark sharp eyes at Cal slumped like putty in the seat of the Mercury. Bentley could see Dakin's look land like a crackling blue flame on Cal's still shape, running over him like lightning. She tried to watch, but she had to close her eyes and cover them with her hands against the brightness of the power.

When she peeked, squinting through her fingers a moment later, there were a few last flickers and sparks flying over him as Cal's eyes sprang open. He took a deep breath, stretched, and jumped to his feet.

"Yay!" Bentley couldn't help it. She was so glad to see him up and moving that she started clapping and beaming like an idiot.

"Way to go!" Arthur said.

Dakin waved a hand, inviting Cal to join them.

"This is Dakin," Bentley told him as he trotted up.

"I know. I heard everything." Cal was studying the tall, white-haired man. "Why did you hang around being Klack? And why did you go away in the first place? Mordicus couldn't figure it out at all. And he never said so, but I think his feelings were really hurt when you left him like that."

"Hmm." Dakin's face furrowed. "I suppose I should have given him some explanation. The thing is, I was having my own dark days and not thinking clearly. I'd had too much power and too much experience myself. Burned out. I just ran away."

"Where did you go?" Cal asked. "Mordicus said he looked everywhere for you."

Dakin's frown softened with pleasant memories. "I spent the first hundred years or so as a rock. It's a very quiet, slow kind of life. Peaceful. Later I became a tree. Also very pleasant. After some years, when I was thoroughly rested, I began to get curious about what was going on in the world I had left. I wanted

to find my star pupil and see what he'd made of himself." Dakin made a face. "Very disappointing. If
Mordicus was the best I could do as a teacher, I
thought, I might as well stay a raven."

"But you're back to yourself," Bentley pointed
out. "Are you going to stay?"

Dakin's eyebrows rose, and one hand tugged at his
long white beard. "There's a lot that needs doing and
undoing here, thanks to Mordicus. And I do feel well-
rested and ready to work. I think I will stay, at least
until I need more time as a rock."

The turtle's head crept once more out of its shell,
and Mordicus blinked up at his former master.

Forlorn, Bentley thought. Good word. And exactly how Mordicus looked right now.

Dakin looked at the turtle and then at Cal. "You
should have a pet," he said.

Cal's eyes widened. "A pet?"

"A turtle makes a nice, quiet pet," Dakin said.
"Not much bother, although he'll be quite dependent
on you. You'll decide if he goes for a swim, if he eats
grubs or strawberries and pizza, if he gets out to see
the world or stays in a small glass tank."

"Oh," Cal said softly. "I see."

"Our friend Mordicus must learn what it's like to
be helpless," Dakin said. "It'll be good for him to
know what it's like to depend on someone else. And
as a turtle, slow moving and built close to the ground,
he'll simply have to learn patience and humility. Excellent lessons." Dakin bent to direct his words at
Mordicus's shell. "Hear that? Patience and humility!"

"I'll take good care of him," Cal said.

"Of course you will," Dakin agreed. "That's the kind of person you are. I suppose there was some remnant of decency left in Mordicus to recognize it."

Everything was working out perfectly, Bentley thought. Cal, Charles, and James Francis would all be fine. "Hey! What about Dr. Gardner? I think Mordicus put some kind of spell on him. And Dr. Craven's mixed up in it somehow, trying to get Dr. Gardner in trouble. Can you help him?"

"Leave it to Mordicus to get together with a weasel like Craven," Dakin said. "It definitely needs undoing."

"We found Craven asleep in the hall outside the turret room when we rescued Charles and James Francis," Arthur said. "We didn't know why he was there, so we just left him."

Dakin tapped his nose thoughtfully. "Sound reasoning. As far as I know, he wasn't expected. I think it's most likely that Craven had come skulking around to ask for something and simply got caught in the sleeping spell with your brothers."

"There's a faculty meeting today!" Bentley remembered. "The university is putting Dr. Gardner on trial to see if he's really crazy. I'll bet Dr. Craven wanted help with that!"

"We'll see," Dakin said. "Come on!" He led the way to the black Coupe de Ville with Bentley, Arthur, and Cal on his heels. They left Mordicus on his back in the road. Dakin threw open the Cadillac's heavy black door. Inside, the limp, snoring body of Dr.

Craven, still dressed in his long dark coat and floppy hat, sprawled across the backseat of the car.

"Now, then, Craven, what's all this about?" Dakin demanded.

Dr. Craven caught himself with a snort in mid-snore. His eyes were still closed as he answered in a whining, singsong voice, as if he were talking in his sleep. "I'll show them! I'm smarter than any of them!"

Dakin *tsked* and rolled his eyes.

"All I need is a little help getting rid of that old man," Dr. Craven whined. "Please?"

Dakin shook his head in disgust. "Go back and be exactly who you are. There's no help for you here."

With a puff of sour-smelling yellow smoke, Dr. Craven disappeared.

Bentley sneezed. "And what about the way Dr. Gardner gets ferhoodled?"

"Ferhoodled," Dakin repeated. "Good word." He tugged at his beard. "Let's have a look in the back, shall we?"

The white-haired man trotted around the black Cadillac to open the trunk. Inside it was a dusty rubble of equipment, tools, screws, bolts, and springs, battered toasters, mixers, and a wide assortment of very odd clocks.

Dakin snorted. "Nasty stuff, all of it." He waved a hand over the trunk and said a word clean as a tree. Lights in all colors crackled and flared over the rusty, dusty parts until the trunk was snapping and sparking like fireworks. Bentley, Arthur, and Cal jumped away from the spray of sparks while Dakin stood frowning and shaking his head.

A few minutes later, the sparks had finally died. "There!" Dakin said. "At least it's a beginning, but we've got a lot more to do!" The white-haired man turned his dark eyes on Cal. "Are you done with magic, Cal, or would you like to study with me?"

It didn't take Cal long to decide. "I'd like it a lot!"

"Good!" Then Dakin turned to Bentley. "And what about you?"

"Me?" Her voice squeaked.

"Certainly." Dakin's quick duck of the head was a Klack-like nod. "You have a natural talent for handling power."

"Say yes!" Cal urged. His eyes were shining.

"Um," Bentley said. Power? Talent? Did she really have that? She thought of the wonder of her lion and slowly nodded. "Yes!"

"Excellent!" Dakin winked at his two new pupils.

It was going to be quite a summer, Bentley thought. Later, she'd have to think of a word for it. A lot of words.

"What time is it?" Arthur suddenly asked. "It must be really late!"

"Time to move on," Dakin said in a brisk and gentle voice. "Time to move on."

19

There were lights on all over the house when Bentley got home, and one of her mom's favorite opera records was booming from the dining room. She could hear her mom in the kitchen singing along to the "Toreador Song" from *Carmen*. It was a scratchy old record and a silly song, but there was still something grand and proud about it, and it seemed like the perfect song to come home to when you were feeling heroic.

Bentley began to sing along as she marched to the kitchen. She posed dramatically in the doorway, and her mom joined her, singing and waving a wooden spoon covered in orange-yellow rice. They both swaggered around the kitchen toreador-style, coming to a loudly satisfying finish together.

When the song ended, they applauded themselves and took turns bowing to each other. It was the end of the record, and they filled the silence with noise and laughter.

"Some of those opera songs aren't too bad," Bentley said.

"I'm glad you think so!" her mom said. "I guess you're getting into all kinds of art appreciation now—such as your face paint. Very interesting."

Face paint? Bentley's hands flew to her cheeks and then her forehead, feeling something soft and gritty under her fingers. Uncle Rudy's red dust! She had forgotten she was still wearing it. But before Bentley could come up with an explanation, her mom explained it for herself.

"You must have been playing Indians. You haven't done that in years!" Her mom smiled as if she were glad to see Bentley regressing. "But you might want to get cleaned up a bit. Rudy and Dr. Gardner will be here anytime now."

"You mean the hearing is over already?" Bentley was astonished. It seemed like no time at all since she had seen Dr. Craven snoring away in the world between the cracks. But, Bentley thought, maybe time was as uncertain as geography in that strange place.

Her mom didn't answer. She had shifted her attention to the cast-iron Dutch oven on the stove.

Bentley moved closer to take a cautious look at what her mom was stirring. "What is that?"

"Seafood paella. From that new place, Alejandro's. We're having a Spanish night, *comprende*? *Carmen* and *paella*!"

"What's in there exactly?" Bentley was looking

suspiciously at some rubbery gray hunks mixed with the orange-yellow rice.

"Octopus!" Her mom poked a gray hunk with her spoon. "Squid too. Plus shrimp, assorted vegetables, and some other things. Alejandro himself told me it was very authentic."

Bentley could see little round suckers on some of the rubbery gray hunks. Tentacles!

"Worry about the squid later," her mom said. "Right now you ought to be getting cleaned up."

Bentley took a quick bath and had just finished dressing when she heard the crash of the back door announce Uncle Rudy's arrival. She rushed down the stairs and into the kitchen in time to hear him play a grand finale fanfare on a yellow-and-red kazoo.

As the last buzzing notes ended, Bentley and her mom clapped and cheered. "Hurray! Bravo!"

"Good news?" Bentley's mom was smiling hopefully.

"The worst." Uncle Rudy grinned. "I'm stuck with Gardner for at least another twenty years!"

"What?" Bentley blinked at him.

"The verdict was definitely Not Crazy. And," Uncle Rudy added gleefully, "the dean actually called Craven a nincompoop. Ha!"

Bentley cheered. She and her mom and Uncle Rudy all pounded one another on the back in congratulations.

"Craven was half an hour late arriving," Uncle Rudy said. "He came catapulting into the meeting wearing an old raincoat and hat, looking like a fugitive from a cheap spy novel. Then he made a complete idiot out of himself. And Gardner," Uncle Rudy said proudly, "was dignified, wise, gracious, and not the least bit ferhoodled even once!"

"Where is Dr. Gardner?" Bentley's mom asked. "He's with you, isn't he?"

"He was right behind me, but he got bogged down enjoying himself again at the night-blooming tobacco. But because Gardner is carrying tonight's champagne, I think I'll go hurry him along. Or at least relieve him of his burden." Uncle Rudy headed for the back door, accompanying himself on the kazoo.

Bentley decided later that paella would go on her "fairly edible" list. It was pretty good as long as you didn't eat any tentacles.

After dinner, Dr. Gardner and Uncle Rudy made toasts in Swahili, Gaelic, Chinese, and other unpronounceable languages. Then Bentley's mom jumped to her feet. "I propose a toast to Right Triumphant!" she cried.

Uncle Rudy jumped up and raised his glass. "To courage!" he said with a little bow to Bentley and a gigantic wink.